NOT DEAD YET

EVA RAE THOMAS MYSTERY - BOOK 7

WILLOW ROSE

Books by the Author

HARRY HUNTER MYSTERY SERIES

- All The Good Girls
- Run Girl Run
- No Other Way
- Never Walk Alone

MARY MILLS MYSTERY SERIES

- What Hurts the Most
- You Can Run
- You Can't Hide
- Careful Little Eyes

EVA RAE THOMAS MYSTERY SERIES

- Don't Lie to me
- What you did
- Never Ever
- Say You Love me
- Let Me Go
- It's Not Over
- Not Dead yet

EMMA FROST SERIES

- Itsy Bitsy Spider
- Miss Dolly had a Dolly
- Run, Run as Fast as You Can
- Cross Your Heart and Hope to Die
- Peek-a-Boo I See You
- Tweedledum and Tweedledee

- Easy as One, Two, Three
- There's No Place like Home
- Slenderman
- Where the Wild Roses Grow
- Waltzing Mathilda
- Drip Drop Dead
- Black Frost

JACK RYDER SERIES

- Hit the Road Jack
- Slip out the Back Jack
- The House that Jack Built
- Black Jack
- Girl Next Door
- Her Final Word
- Don't Tell

REBEKKA FRANCK SERIES

- One, Two...He is Coming for You
- Three, Four...Better Lock Your Door
- Five, Six...Grab your Crucifix
- Seven, Eight...Gonna Stay up Late
- Nine, Ten...Never Sleep Again
- Eleven, Twelve...Dig and Delve
- Thirteen, Fourteen...Little Boy Unseen
- Better Not Cry
- Ten Little Girls
- It Ends Here

MYSTERY/THRILLER/HORROR NOVELS

- Sorry Can't Save You
- In One Fell Swoop
- Umbrella Man

- Blackbird Fly
- To Hell in a Handbasket
- Edwina

HORROR SHORT-STORIES

- Mommy Dearest
- The Bird
- Better watch out
- Eenie, Meenie
- Rock-a-Bye Baby
- Nibble, Nibble, Crunch
- Humpty Dumpty
- Chain Letter

PARANORMAL SUSPENSE/ROMANCE NOVELS

- In Cold Blood
- The Surge
- Girl Divided

THE VAMPIRES OF SHADOW HILLS SERIES

- Flesh and Blood
- Blood and Fire
- Fire and Beauty
- Beauty and Beasts
- Beasts and Magic
- Magic and Witchcraft
- Witchcraft and War
- War and Order
- Order and Chaos
- Chaos and Courage

THE AFTERLIFE SERIES

- Beyond

- Serenity
- Endurance
- Courageous

THE WOLFBOY CHRONICLES

- A Gypsy Song
- I am WOLF

DAUGHTERS OF THE JAGUAR

- Savage
- Broken

Prologue

Merritt Island, Florida

"THERE WE GO. They're at it again."

Mrs. Berkeley put her finger gently on the drapes and pulled them aside, just enough to peek out, but not so much that she might be seen from the street. Her eyes landed on the beautiful Victorian house across from her on Old Settlement Road. Their road was a small dead-end street on the island, in a secluded and exclusive part of Merritt Island, with only about ten houses that almost never got on the market. Mrs. Berkeley knew everyone who lived there very well, as some families had been there through several generations. She was especially fond of the couple living across the street from her in the pink house with the wrap-around porches. But their fighting lately had been getting on her nerves.

"Can you believe them? Fighting again like this," she said to her Miniature Schnauzer, Daisy, who stared at her with big brown eyes, but mostly at the cookie in her hand that she expected to get a bite of soon, as usual.

Mrs. Berkeley broke off a piece of the cookie and fed it to the dog. It almost snapped it out of her hand, then gulped it down before it continued to stare at her with its very brown eyes that she couldn't say no to.

"What is happening to this street and the people?" she said, while she peered over there once again as someone yelled loudly. Mrs. Berkeley let go of the drape with a small snort. "Well, it's none of our business, is it, Daisy? No, it isn't."

The dog lifted its paw and begged for another piece, and Mrs. Berkeley caved. The voices rose from across the street, and Mrs. Berkeley got a nervous sensation in her chest. This was a nice street. People didn't usually yell at one another, especially not so loud that the neighbors could hear it.

"I sure hope they're not going to get a divorce," Mrs. Berkeley said, a hand to her chest to calm her pounding heart. She never liked it when people fought. She and her husband, Dr. Berkeley, most certainly had never yelled at one another like that. They could disagree on things, absolutely. And if he misbehaved, Mrs. Berkeley would give him the silent treatment for days until he caved. That was how it was done back in her day. Civilized and educated people didn't yell or fight.

"Those poor children."

Daisy answered with a pant, sticking her tongue out, while Mrs. Berkeley ate the rest of the cookie. Seeing it disappear into Mrs. Berkeley's mouth, the dog laid down on the couch, head resting on its paws.

"Now, I never," Mrs. Berkeley exclaimed as a loud noise sounded from across the street. She put her finger on the drape and pulled it aside again. "It sounds almost like they're fighting. And who is that yelling so loudly? Tsk."

She stared out the window at the driveway where Mrs. Henry's nice new Tesla was parked just as the garage door opened, and someone staggered outside.

"Nancy?" Mrs. Berkeley said, staring at the woman running down the driveway, squinting her eyes to better see in the darkness. "My Goodness, dear Nancy, why are you running like that?"

It was her. Mrs. Berkeley was almost certain, even though it was hard to see. Nancy was so elegant, even when running. Why was she running? She seemed almost like she was scared? But what could have frightened her so?

Pulse quickening, Mrs. Berkeley held her breath as she saw the shadow come up behind Nancy. Moving swiftly through the darkness, the shadow grabbed her by the ponytail from behind and yanked her back forcefully. Nancy let out a scream that made Mrs. Berkeley's heart jump as her legs shot out underneath her, and she landed on the pavement before she was dragged, kicking and screaming, back inside the house.

Seeing this, Mrs. Berkeley let go of the drape and took a step away from the window. Sweat sprang to her upper lip, which she had recently had botoxed. A tic grew evident near her eye as she stared at the window, heart beating fast in her chest.

Then she shook her head. "It's none of our business, Daisy, dear. It really isn't."

She turned to walk away while she could hear Nancy screaming:

"Stop it. Stop!"

That's when she decided to have that brandy after all, even though she was trying to cut down on the late-night alcohol. She had just grabbed the bottle from the shelf when the shot echoed through the neighborhood.

It wasn't the first time Mrs. Berkeley drank an entire bottle of brandy before bedtime, but it was the first time she drank it straight from the bottle.

Part I

FIVE YEARS LATER

Sykes Creek, Merritt Island, Florida

Chapter 1

"IS this the right way to do it, Dad?"

Bryan Nelson looked at his son, Max, holding the shrimp between his fingers while putting it on the hook. Bryan couldn't help but smile. He had wanted to take his son fishing for as long as he could remember, but his wife had told him no. After being in an accident as a child, Terri was terrified of boats and didn't want her kid out on one of them. Ever. There was nothing Bryan could say or do to make her change her mind, and during his upbringing, she had instilled her fears into the boy, making him scared of anything to do with water and especially boats.

Now, they were separated, and Bryan had decided to take the boy fishing. Bryan had fished all his life and held some of his dearest memories with his late father doing just that. Why rob his son of that? Bryan was only sad that he had waited so long to do it. He had listened to Terri for way too long, and in that way, missed out on many great adventures and hours spent with his son.

It was time to change that now—time to make memories that would last them both a lifetime.

"Yes, that's perfect, son," he said. "Now, watch me as I cast first, and I'll help you cast yours too, okay?"

The boy gleamed up at his father, then nodded. Bryan cast his line, and it plopped in the water far away.

"Whoooa," the boy exclaimed when seeing how far his dad had thrown the line. His big eyes stared up at him, and Bryan felt like a superhero. It wasn't a feeling he had experienced a lot in his time as a father. Terri had always told him he was worthless and that he could do nothing right. And maybe it was true. Bryan hadn't accomplished much in life if you looked at it from the outside. He still worked in the same boat shop he had as a teenager when it was just a part-time job. But that was only because he really enjoyed it. He liked helping people finding the right boat for them. And he absolutely loved being out on the water himself, and these were people who shared that same passion. His passion for boating and fishing made him the best salesman the store had, and the owner, old Hubbard, had told him if he kept this up, he might let him take over the store once he decided to retire. He didn't have a son, and Bryan was the closest he had to one.

"Now, it's your turn," Bryan said with a sniffle. He walked up behind his son and helped grab the pole between his small hands, then slung the line out in the still water, where the hook with the shrimp plunged in.

"That was a pretty good throw there, son," he said, patting the boy on the shoulder. That made the boy stand up straight with pride. He was getting so tall, and soon he'd be taller than his father. This was the time to enjoy him, to bond. In a few years, it would be too late.

Bryan was going to get in trouble for taking the boy fishing today. He was supposed to be in school. Terri was going to rip his head off when she found out. Yet, he did it anyway. This was his only chance. If he asked first, he knew the answer. Terri wasn't the boss of him anymore. Max was his son too.

"So, now we wait and keep an eye on the pole, okay, son?" he asked. "Let me know if it starts moving."

The boy nodded. Bryan grabbed a juice box from the cooler and handed it to him. It was a hot one out today. Important to stay hydrated. Bryan grabbed a beer for himself and sat back, pulling his cap down a little to better cover his face from the scorching sun. It was a nice day to be out on the water. The fish were jumping around them, and there were no other sounds except for the occasional heron that would take off, squawking.

This is the life. Nothing better than this. Right here.

Bryan closed his eyes and sipped his beer, enjoying this moment. Barely had the sizzling sensation of the beer hitting his stomach settled before he heard his son gasp lightly, then say:

"What's that?'

Bryan opened his eyes and looked at the boy. He was pointing out at the water. "What's what, boy?"

"There's something in the water. Something big."

Thinking it might be a tarpon or maybe even a bull shark, Bryan rose to his feet and approached the edge of the boat where Max was standing.

"Let me see where?" Bryan asked.

"Over there. That red thing."

Bryan felt disappointment as he stared at the red thing on the surface. At first, it looked like a piece of wood or a big lump of seaweed, but the color was wrong. You didn't see that kind of bright red color in nature. What worried Bryan the most was how the mass seemed to bob up and down. And as it surfaced again, he believed for a second that it might be a piece of fabric, maybe a jacket someone had lost from the bridge on 520 nearby, or perhaps from a boat. It disappeared again, pulled by the current, then resurfaced closer to them, and that's when Bryan realized it was more than just a jacket or a shirt. It was something bigger. It kept bobbing up, then disappearing underwater, and that's when Bryan knew exactly what it was. He had seen this before, in his time serving in the coast guard. They had been sent out to that plane crash—a small aircraft that had crashed into the water with a family of four inside it. They had pulled that first body out of the water, burnt beyond recognition, and he still dreamt about it at night.

"What is it, Daddy? What is it? Is it a fish?" Max asked, his voice growing excited. "Is it a big shark, maybe?"

Bryan grabbed the boy by the shoulders and pulled him away from the edge. "No, son. It's not."

"Then, what is it? Daddy?"

Bryan swallowed and grabbed a paddle as the mass came closer, and he was able to reach out for it. He touched it and, as it moved, the long brown hair swayed in the water.

Seeing this, Bryan took off his cap and shirt, then jumped in.

Chapter 2

"I'M FAT!"

I stared at myself in the mirror that I had accidentally looked at myself in when walking by. We were in Target, Matt and I, and were supposed to be buying baby stuff for the nursery. But now I didn't want to go any further. I just wanted to cry.

Matt came up behind me and touched my stomach. "You're not fat, Eva Rae."

I nodded. "Yes, I am. Look at me. I look awful."

"I think you're beautiful," he smiled.

"Well, you don't count."

"Oh, really? And why is that?"

I sulked. "Because you're biased."

He let go of me. "Okay, how about this, then? Yes, you're fat, Eva Rae."

"Geez, thanks," I said.

He grabbed my face between his hands. I wanted to punch him and kiss him at the same time. I guess my hormones were wacky as usual these days.

"You're supposed to be fat, remember? You're expecting."

"Please, don't use that expression," I said. "It makes me feel like I'm eighty. Or that you are. It also makes me want to gag."

Matt laughed and let go of me. I smiled with a shrug, then touched my belly. I was still at the stage where you couldn't really tell if I was pregnant or had just gained a lot of weight. And I had gained a lot—more than with any of my other three children at this point. The pregnancy had been harder on me as well. I was more tired and felt more nauseated than in my earlier pregnancies.

Maybe I was just too old for this. Being pregnant at forty-two wasn't exactly ideal.

Matt placed a hand on my stomach and kissed me. "I can't wait to hold our baby in my arms."

I sighed. Matt had one other child, Elijah, but he hadn't been a part of the boy's baby years. He had gotten a woman pregnant, and she decided not to tell him until the child was three years old. He had missed out on a lot that he hoped to make up for now, but I feared he'd be scared away. He had no idea how hard it was to have a little infant in your life. He hadn't gone through the sleepless nights or the crying for hours on end. He hadn't had a hormonal woman in his life, yelling at him one minute, then wanting to make passionate love to him the next. I feared he was in for a bit of a surprise. Luckily, I had done it three times before. Oliva was now fifteen, Christine thirteen, and Alex seven, and I feared I had forgotten just how hard it was. I thought I was done with this part of my life and wasn't sure I could deal with another time around. This wasn't just the baby years, with the waking up every hour to eat or the constant changing of diapers, there'd be the terrible toddler years where you didn't have a second to think, and then all the other stuff that I had probably forgotten about. I felt like I had enough dealing with two teenage girls in my life, driving me nuts. Adding a baby on top of it?

It was spelling disaster.

"I like this one over here," he said and pointed at a crib. "Doesn't that look like one he—or she—could sleep in all night, huh? It sure looks comfortable."

"Matt, it's five hundred bucks. You must be crazy."

"But it's the best one here. Nothing's too good for our baby, right?

We want her—or him—to be comfortable in the bed, so he'll sleep all night, right?"

I sighed and put my hand on his shoulder. "You do realize the baby is never going to sleep in that thing, right? I'll be feeding him or her all night, and then eventually, the baby will end up sleeping in our bed. That's what happened to all of my other three children."

Matt looked dumfounded. "But...how will we avoid lying on top of her or him? I'm a heavy sleeper."

"Oh, don't worry, you won't be sleeping in the bed. You'll probably be in the guestroom, so you can take the baby in the morning in order to give me a couple of hours of sleep."

Matt stared at me, mouth gaping. I hated to make him feel like he was oblivious, but I needed to be honest right away, so he wouldn't be disappointed. Having a baby was no joke, and a comfortable—very expensive—bed was no guarantee for a good night's rest. There was only one thing we could be certain of, and that was that it was going to be hard work.

Chapter 3

THEN:

"Hey, what's with the long face?"

Jade looked up from her phone with a sniffle. She wiped her nose with the back of her hand, then shook her head. It was Billy who had asked. He was a close friend of her parents, and right now, he was helping them by fixing the sink in the kitchen.

"I'm sorry," she said. "I didn't know you were here."

Billy was going through his toolbox and pulled out a wrench. "Your mom called. Said you had water coming out this morning. She couldn't get ahold of a plumber who could make it out today, so I said I would do it."

"Oh, yeah," Jade said, remembering the chaotic morning they'd had before school. Their dad was away for the week, as he often was as a traveling salesman. Billy was his best friend since high school. He lived close by and was her mom's go-to guy when Jade's dad was away.

"So, what's up?" he asked.

"What do you mean?"

"You looked really sad when you walked in while looking at that phone of yours."

Jade shrugged, then put down the phone. She walked to the fridge and opened it.

"Just some friend stuff."

He nodded, still holding the wrench in hand. "I see. Friends can be a bummer, huh? Especially at your age. I remember my sister always having trouble with hers. One day she went to school, and her best friend for years had turned her back on her and was now best friends with someone else. Just like that. I never understood how girls could be so mean to one another in middle school."

"Yeah, well, I am a freshman now in high school. Things were supposed to be different," Jade said and pulled out the milk. "At least I always thought it would be. But the drama this year is awful. It makes me sick."

Billy nodded. "Yeah, well, it used to make my sister sick too."

"I try to stay out of it, but they keep dragging me in, and I don't like it," she said. "I don't really have many friends and stay mostly to myself in school."

"What?" Billy said. "A girl like you doesn't have many friends? That can't be true."

"Well, it is. No one likes me at school."

"I'm sure the boys do. They must be lining up to date you, right?"

That made Jade laugh. "Not really. They prefer the popular girls, and I am not one of those."

"They must be nuts," Billy said with a wink. "A girl like you back in my day would have been very popular." He shook his head. "Kids these days."

Jade poured herself a glass of milk, then drank it. She felt Billy's eyes on her, and it made her blush. She realized she had a milk mustache and wiped it away. She approached the sink and looked down at him as he crawled in underneath it again with the wrench in his hand.

"So, what's wrong?" she said, leaning in above him. "With the sink?"

He looked up at her, then smiled. "It's nothing really. I just need to change a gasket. It'll be done in a jiff, and I'll be out of your hair."

Jade shrugged again. She didn't mind having Billy at the house. On the contrary, she preferred him over an empty house. She never liked coming home and being all alone in the big dark house. Her brother Ethan wouldn't be home till after football practice in two hours, and her mother had said she would be home right before dinner. Jade was always alone in the house for several hours, and she hated that. Especially after the neighbors had their car broken into, it freaked her out. Having Billy there made her feel safer. He was tall and strong, and he was a cop.

"So, how do you do that? Change...what did you call it, a gasket?" she asked.

He lifted his head and looked at her, a gleam in his eyes. "You want me to teach you?"

She shrugged again. "Sure. Why not? Beats doing homework."

"All right," he said. "Lie down next to me here on the floor, and I'll show you. You might get your clothes wet or dirty. Are you sure you're okay with that?"

"Of course."

Chapter 4

"WE'RE GOING to need a baby monitor, right?" Matt asked and held one up that looked like it could communicate with our baby on the moon. I stared at the monster in Matt's hands, then smiled.

"Sure. But a simpler one would do. Our kid isn't going out in space anytime soon."

He put it down, then looked at another one. I sensed he was a little angry with me, and I placed my hand on his shoulder.

"Are you okay?"

"Yeah, I'm fine. It's just..."

"What? Matt, look at me. What is it?"

He turned around to face me. "It's gonna sound silly, but it sort of feels like you're not really into this. Not really."

"What do you mean I'm *not into it*? Have you seen my fat stomach? I'm in so deep that I can't see my feet anymore."

"There you go again, making fun of me," Matt said. "I could barely get you to do this with me today. You kept postponing this shopping trip. I've been looking forward to this for so long, and you don't want to buy anything. It's like you don't even want this child. This is our first child together. It's my first baby."

I looked at Matt, then felt ashamed. He was right. I wasn't into this as much as he was. I sighed and rubbed my face, feeling how swollen my fingers were. I was only five months pregnant and already feeling the toll on my body. It was going to be a long pregnancy.

"Matt, I am into it. It's just…well, it's my fourth child. And I wasn't exactly planning on having another one, so, yes, it has taken me a while to get used to the thought. And maybe I didn't really want another baby at first. You're so right about that, but…"

I was mid-sentence when Matt's phone rang. He pulled it out of his pocket. "It's Chief Annie. I need to take this."

"Of course."

Matt put the phone to his ear, and I heard him talk in a low voice for a few seconds while I looked at a mobile. I still had some of Alex's old baby stuff in a box somewhere and felt pretty sure I had a mobile that looked a lot like this one in it. The truth was, I wanted to buy new stuff, but I also wanted to save money. Having a new baby in the house was going to be expensive. I didn't feel that Matt was being realistic about it and wanted to spend too much money upfront on things we probably wouldn't need.

Matt came back and handed me the phone. "It's for you."

"For me?"

"Chief Annie wants to talk to you," Matt said.

"Really?"

He gave me a look, and I grabbed the phone. "Hi, Chief, what's up?"

"We need you, Eva Rae. I just got off the phone with the sheriff's office, and they wanted me to get in contact with you."

"So, you called Matt?"

"Well, I needed to get ahold of both of you. Because of your condition, I'm sending Matt with you. He can assist you, so you don't overexert yourself. I want you both on this case."

"Case, but…hey, wait a minute. I don't work anymore, remember? I quit."

Annie sighed. "You're the only one around here with enough experience. The sheriff's office is in over their head. We need your expertise on this. Please, Eva Rae?"

Chapter 5

"I THINK YOU SHOULD SAY NO."

Matt stared at me. His eyes were determined. "You're in no condition to take a case right now. You need rest."

"It's not like I'm sick, Matt. I'm pregnant. You act like I am dying. With Alex, I worked until the day I gave birth. My water literally broke while at the office. He turned out fine. I don't need you acting like I'm sick, okay?"

"You're older now," Matt said.

My eyes grew wide. "Excuse me? What did you just say?"

He threw out his arms. "It's the truth, isn't it? You're forty-two. There are a lot of risks involved with having a child this late in life."

"Matt, look at me," I said and grabbed his collar, then pulled him close so he could look into my eyes. "I am not too old to have a child or to work, do you hear me? No matter what the Internet says. Our child is not at risk."

I was so angry I was almost spitting. The day before, Sydney and I had been to a trailer park and liberated two young girls who were being held there by traffickers. I had beat one of them up pretty badly. I couldn't help myself. He had been bent over one of the girls when we got there, kicking her in the face while laughing. I had knocked him down with the grip of my gun, then punched him a few times. He was passed out when we left, and I called the cops on them on account of the drugs we had seen lying around the place.

All this I had done while pregnant, but, of course, Matt didn't know anything about it. All he knew was that my sister Sydney and I ran a rescue place, a shelter for trafficked girls, where they could be nurtured back to life. What he didn't know was that sometimes we took it upon ourselves to liberate them when things needed to move quickly. It was dangerous and maybe even stupid in my condition, but it had to be done.

I wanted to tell Matt about it, to let him know I was every bit as strong as I was before I had this baby planted in me. But I didn't. I knew he'd worry and get angry. I didn't need that right now.

"Well, that's just too bad," I said. "I already said we'd do it."

"You did what? Eva Rae, how can you be so…"

"Yes, Matt? Please, finish that sentence."

His nostrils were flaring as he was composing himself, calming himself. "Sometimes, you really annoy me, Eva Rae."

I smiled gently. "Come on, Matt. It might be fun working together again."

He stared down at me like he wanted to strangle me, then eased up as our eyes locked. He never could say no to me.

"Pretty please?" I said.

"The physical appearance of the please makes no difference," he said with a sigh, quoting from the movie *Despicable Me,* which I always referred to when my kids said that.

It made me laugh. I started to walk toward the exit of the store.

"Let's get going then. They're waiting for us at the hospital."

He growled behind me but caught up quickly.

"I have a feeling I'm going to regret this."

Chapter 6

CAPE CANAVERAL HOSPITAL was no more than ten minutes from the Target we were in. I drove up and parked in front of the tall building that was set on a peninsula, surrounded by water. I had always believed it was a very exclusive location for a hospital, and the views from the top floors were gorgeous. You could see the cruise ships docked at the port on one side, sunsets over the mainland on another, and the ocean on a third. You were completely surrounded by water no matter where you turned to look.

We were directed to a room where Detective Roberts from the sheriff's office greeted us. He was in his mid-fifties. He was a slightly built man but sturdily attractive with winter gray hair and bushy eyebrows over keen, penetrating eyes. I knew him a little from another case we worked on many years ago. He smiled widely.

"Eva Rae Thomas. You are a sight for sore eyes. I knew you'd say yes," he said, shaking my hand excitedly.

"So, you're the reason I was called?" I asked. "I was wondering about that."

He shrugged with a smug smile. "I knew you were around after that thing in Orlando. I thought, who better to help us out?"

Roberts' glance landed on my stomach. He squinted his eyes. "This is one of those times when you have to be careful about saying anything. I've gotten myself in trouble before, but..."

I exhaled deeply. "Yes, I'm pregnant. It's Matt's."

"So, you're the lucky guy," Roberts said with a wink at me. He shook Matt's hand. "Good luck keeping track of this one, ha-ha."

"So, what have we got?" I asked to change the subject before it got too uncomfortable for both Matt and me. Roberts didn't know just how much he had stepped in it. "The chief said you pulled a woman out of Sykes Creek?"

Roberts nodded. "A dad and his son, who had gone fishing for the day, spotted the body in the water. The dad jumped in and pulled her out. He thought she was dead, but as he got her on board the boat, he realized she was alive."

I nodded. "And when did this take place?"

"Yesterday morning. She was brought to the hospital and has been in the care of the doctors since."

Matt cleared his throat. "So, what do you need our help with?"

Roberts looked down briefly, then back up at me, seriousness in his eyes. "The woman's name is Nancy Henry."

Matt's eyes grew wide. "As in the Nancy Henry? Charles Henry's wife?"

Roberts nodded. "That one, yes."

"Let's back up for a second here. What am I missing? Who is Nancy Henry, and why should I know her?"

Matt looked at me. "Nancy Henry disappeared five years ago after a home intrusion. It's been a mystery what happened to her."

"I see. So this woman has been gone for five years, and no one knows where she has been? What is she saying?"

Roberts shook his head. "She doesn't remember a thing."

I lifted both eyebrows. "She doesn't remember where she has been for the past five years?"

He nodded. "She has suffered a blow to the back of her head that fractured her skull before she fell in the water or maybe right when she fell in, and the doctor says it's possible she suffered memory loss due to that."

"Really?" I asked. "And what about her husband? Does she remember him?"

Roberts nodded. "Her husband arrived last night, and apparently she remembers both him and the children, yes."

"What a strange story," I said. "And where do I come in?"

"Well, she was found with a lot of morphine in her blood. Enough to kill her, but miraculously, it didn't. She has bruises on her wrists like she was tied up. And then there is the fractured skull. We believe someone tried to kill her but didn't succeed. Whoever it was must have thought she was dead, then thrown her off the bridge. The fisherman saved her life. Had she been in the water for much longer, she would have drowned. I need you and Matt here to help me investigate what really happened to her. Who took her and later tried to kill her?"

Chapter 7

SO, we're basically chasing a potential murderer and kidnapper of a victim who doesn't even know it happened?

The thought lingered deep in my mind as Matt and I followed Roberts into the hospital room, where Nancy Henry was sitting up in her bed, leaning her bandaged head on the pillow behind her. Even in the state she was in, she was gorgeous. It didn't look like she had lacked having any needs met over the past five years. But looks could be tricky; I knew that much. Pretty girls often had more trouble convincing the doctors they were sick because they didn't look it. Nancy Henry didn't look much like a victim to me as she lifted her head to look at us when we entered. In the corner of the room sat a man in a chair, and I guessed he was Charles Henry. He was darkly handsome with high cheekbones, charcoal brown eyes, and thick black eyebrows. His dark brown hair had touches of gray, but only at the sides. His eyes were red-rimmed from crying, and he seemed agitated and out of sorts. He kept sniffling and wiping his eyes with his hands, then shaking his head.

"We need to talk to Nancy alone now, Charles," Roberts said to him.

He nodded. He was wearing jeans and a white T-shirt, yet

somehow you could just tell he was wealthier than most and had been for his entire life. It was something in the way he carried himself. It was with a certain dignity that most people didn't have.

"We'll probably need to have a chat with you as well, later on," I said as he passed me. He nodded and tried to smile.

"Naturally. I'll be at your disposal anytime."

"Good to hear."

He left, and I approached Nancy in the bed. She gave me a confused and melancholy look.

"This is Eva Rae Thomas," Roberts said, addressed to Nancy. "The former FBI agent that I told you about. She'll be helping us out. We are doing everything we can to find out what happened to you, okay?"

Nancy cleared her throat, then nodded. "Okay. But I really don't have much to add. And I am so tired. Maybe we should wait?"

I glanced at the dark purple bruises on her wrists. "How did you get those? Do you remember?"

She looked at them, then shook her head. "No. As I said, I don't remember anything. It's all just a big darkness, and I can't just switch the light on and suddenly remember it."

"We're here to help you," I said. "There's no need to get defensive."

Nancy scoffed, then placed a hand on her forehead. A tear escaped her eye and rolled down her cheek. "I'm sorry. It's just...a lot right now. I have no idea where I have been or what...and now I wake up here...and then I learn that...I don't even have a husband anymore. I think you'd get defensive too."

I nodded. "Probably. So you're telling me your husband remarried?"

Her hand came down from her forehead and landed on the bedside. More tears rolled down her cheeks. "He thought I was dead."

I grimaced.

"It's like I've been asleep for a really long time and just woke up to a nightmare of a lifetime. Suddenly, I have no husband, and my kids are almost grownups. Five years have passed. Five years? And I don't remember anything."

I grabbed a chair and sat down, beginning to stir up a little sympathy for the woman. It had to be quite the situation to find yourself in.

"Let's start with this then," I said. "Tell me, what is the last thing you remember?"

She gave me a look, then sighed. "The last thing I remember? Well…let's see. I think it is standing in my kitchen. I had made veal for dinner and was expecting Charles home. I don't really remember more than that."

Nancy leaned her head back and made a face that looked like she was in pain. She closed her eyes.

"Listen, I am really tired. Could we do this later? I can barely think straight, let alone remember a lot of stuff."

"And where were the kids?" I asked. "While you were preparing the veal?"

She exhaled, sounding almost annoyed. "Please. I'm just…I don't…"

"Do you recall if they were at home or not?" I asked.

She shook her head, still keeping her eyes closed. "I don't."

"But you remember making veal?"

"Yes. But I don't even know if that was on the day I was kidnapped. It could be a memory from some other day."

"But you know you were kidnapped? How do you know this?" I asked.

"I don't know," she sighed. "I guess I just assumed since the police told me so. They said they believed I was taken from my home by some intruder and kidnapped."

"Do *you* think you were kidnapped?" I asked.

She snorted. "How am I supposed to know? I guess so. I just know what they told me."

"And why do you think they assume you were kidnapped?"

"Because of the bruises on my wrists that look like I've been tied up, or maybe because I was found in the water with a lethal dose of morphine in my blood and a severe blow to the back of my head. Maybe because I was supposed to be dead by now, but somehow like with some stroke of a miracle, I am not," she almost spat and looked at me like I was a complete idiot.

I tried to smile. It came off as annoyed. "Again, I am here to help you—to find out what happened to you."

"It sure doesn't feel like it," she argued. "It feels, frankly, like I am on trial here. I don't know, okay? I don't know anything. How do you think that makes me feel? I've lost five years of my life, five years of my children's lives. I've lost my husband to another woman. Meanwhile, I don't even feel like five years have passed. I feel like it was just yesterday I was living with my babies and was married to a wonderful man. I had everything. In the blink of an eye, I have lost it all. So, I'm sorry if I'm not feeling cheerful and perky right now. My life is in ruins. I don't want to talk to any of you. I don't care if you find those who did this to me or not. I just want my life back, and you can't give me that no matter how many stupid questions you ask me. Now, if you'll excuse me, I need to rest."

With that, Nancy Henry turned around on her side and closed her eyes. Matt and I exchanged a glance, and I signaled for us to leave. Talking to Nancy wasn't getting us anywhere.

At least not for now.

Chapter 8

THEN:

She heard her crying as she walked past her bedroom. The door was left slightly ajar, and Jade couldn't avoid hearing the strong sobs from the other side of it.

"Mom?"

She pressed it gently, and the door slid open. Her mother was lying on the bed, and the sobs stopped when Jade entered.

"Mom? Are you okay?"

Her mother cleared her throat and sat up, turning her face away from her daughter. "I'm fine. It's okay, sweetie. Don't worry."

"But…you're crying, Mom?"

Her mother nodded, then wiped her eyes with her hand before she turned to look at her daughter. She was obviously composing herself for her sake.

"It's nothing, honey. Don't worry about it."

Jade sat down on the side of the bed. "You've been crying a lot lately. Are you sure you're all right?"

Her mother's hand landed on her arm. "I'm fine. It's just… well, life sometimes, you know?"

Jade stared at her mother. She had always believed she was the most beautiful woman in the world, even now that she had been crying. But all children thought that she guessed. Jade didn't always go easy on her, and she knew that. Just this morning, they had been in a huge fight, and Jade had ended up yelling at her that she hated her. But she didn't mean it.

"I'm sorry," she said.

"For what?" her mother asked, surprised.

"For being such a teenager. Am I making you cry?"

Her mother shook her head. "Oh, no, sweetie. You're fine."

"Then, what is it?" Jade kept at it, unable to let it go. "Why are you so upset?"

Her mother scoffed, then shook her head. "I'm just being silly. I think it's my hormones. I feel so wacky half of the time, you know?"

Jade nodded. Yes, she knew all about that. She could barely control herself or her emotions half of the time either. Her mother's eyes suddenly grew serious.

"Life is just hard sometimes. It doesn't always go the way you want it to. And whatever you do, think twice before you marry, okay? Make sure he's the right one for you."

Jade nodded when a voice came from downstairs.

"Knock, knock. Hello? Is anyone home?"

Her mother grimaced. "It's Billy. He can't see me like this."

Her mother jumped out of bed and ran into the bathroom, where she heard her wash her face and take out her makeup kit.

Billy soon poked his face inside the bedroom. His face lit up when he saw Jade. He was in uniform, holding his hat between his hands. The sight of the gun in his belt made Jade wince, partly in fear and partly in excitement.

"Well, hello there, sweetheart. What are you doing in here? Is your mom not home?"

Jade blushed, then looked down. Billy was so handsome, and he had that glint in his eyes. The way he looked at her made her feel warm.

"She's in the bathroom."

The door opened, and her mother came out. She pretended to be surprised by the sight of Billy. She corrected her hair and bit her glossy lip.

"Oh, it's you. What's up?"

What's up?

Jade almost dropped her jaw. Her mother had never used that expression before. As in ever. And was she blushing?

"I was just checking in on my favorite ladies. There has been a break-in in a vehicle two blocks down and wanted to warn you to lock up at night."

"That is sweet of you, Billy. Thank you. We'll remember to lock up. We always do."

"That's great. Say, is that chicken that I smell?"

Jade's mother nodded.

"Oh, you make the best chicken in the world," he said.

"You should stay for dinner," her mother said. "Please, do. We'd love to have you. Right, Jade? Tell Billy how much we'd love for him to stay. We have more than enough food."

Her mother looked at Jade, who lowered her eyes shyly.

"Sure."

Her mother clasped her hands together. "It's decided then. You'll stay for dinner. I won't take no for an answer."

Billy threw out his hands with a smirk. "Guess I'm staying then."

Chapter 9

"I THOUGHT SHE WAS DEAD."

Charles Henry looked up at us from his chair. We were sitting in the waiting area outside Nancy's hospital room while she was sleeping. Charles fumbled nervously with a plastic cup between his hands. It was empty, and it made an annoying noise.

"I truly believed she was dead. Or I wouldn't have married Tanya. And now what? What am I supposed to do?"

I stared at the man in front of me, unable to answer. I couldn't blame him for being out of it. Finding out your wife is alive after five years when you thought she was dead had to be confusing.

"How long have you and Tanya been married?" I asked.

"Four months. We had to wait until we could declare Nancy legally dead after five years of going missing."

"But you dated for longer than that, I take it?" I asked.

"Yes. For a long time, I hoped and prayed that Nancy was still alive," he continued. "But even the police said they believed she was dead. Tanya was my secretary at the time. She helped me through it, and we fell in love. It wasn't like it was planned. It just happened. But does that mean that I'm married to two women now?"

"I don't know the technicalities," I said.

"I'm pretty sure your last marriage will be annulled," Matt argued. "But you might need to look into that at some point."

Charles rubbed his face with a groan. "Why is this happening now? Couldn't she have come back a year ago? Then I wouldn't have remarried. Now, everything is complicated. How do I explain this to Tanya? What do I do? I mean, I didn't do anything wrong, did I? In remarrying?"

"Not legally," I said. "But Nancy might see it differently since in her mind you're still married."

"Argh," he groaned and leaned back in his chair, squeezing the plastic cup tightly. "Just when things seemed to settle down for us. Just when life was getting good again. This happens."

"You almost sound like you're not happy that she's back?" I asked, puzzled.

He looked at me. "Of course, I'm happy that she's back. Are you kidding me? I have waited for this moment for five years. I'm ecstatic. It's just that... well, a lot has changed since she left, including my love for her. I am in love with someone else now, and I can't just turn that off. It's not like there's a switch you can flip, you know? But how do I explain that to Nancy? And to be honest, I can feel myself getting a little angry with her. Is that wrong of me? I feel upset that she doesn't remember where she has been or that time has passed."

"Do you think she might not be telling the truth?" I asked.

He shook his head. "No, no. Nancy isn't someone to lie like that. It's just...well, I would really like to know what happened to her. To better understand her. You know? Oh, I'm not making much sense here. It's been hectic the past twenty-four hours. You'll have to excuse me for babbling like this. I'm usually a much more composed man."

"I'm sure," I said. "But now that we have you, I'd like to go over the night that Nancy disappeared with you."

"Oh, no. I've told this story a gazillion times to you people," he said, running a hand through his hair. "Can't you just read the old reports?"

"I'll do that too, but I'd like to hear it from you as well. There might be something the investigators missed back then. If you don't mind."

Chapter 10

"I STAYED LATE at the office, even though I knew that Nancy had prepared a nice dinner for us. I just couldn't leave."

Charles sighed nervously, then looked up at me.

"Was Tanya your secretary at this point?" I asked.

He nodded. "You mean, were we already having an affair then?"

"Yes."

"We weren't. Tanya and I grew close after Nancy disappeared, not before. I am not that kind of man."

"Okay," I said. "But did Nancy maybe suspect that you were with another woman? Was she jealous?"

That made Charles stop to think. "Come to think of it; she might have been. She did ask me occasionally if I had another woman when I came home late."

"So, she could have believed you were cheating on her even if you weren't," I said.

"I guess so."

"All right. Now, back to the day she disappeared. You were at the office, and she was making dinner, thinking you'd be home on time. Then what?"

I was stuck with a ton of paperwork that needed to be done, clients that I needed to get back to, stuff like that, so I texted her to let her know. She wrote me back that she was disappointed and that dinner would be ruined."

"And what did you answer to that?"

"I might have been a little harsh. I told her I was working and that whether or not dinner got cold was of little importance. In harsher words, perhaps, but you get the picture."

"So, you basically told her what she was angry about was of no importance," I said. "Women love to hear that."

He sighed. "I know. You don't have to tell me that. But I was dealing with some real trouble with a client that couldn't wait. When sitting with that, it was hard for me to worry about whether or not I would make it home for dinner."

"Go on. What time did you leave the office?"

"At ten-thirty," he said. "I drove directly home. I let myself in, and that's when I saw it. The house was a mess like there had been a fight in the living room, which I believe there had been. There was blood on the floor. Nancy was nowhere to be found. I called the police, and they arrived shortly after. And that's basically it. The police later found out that the intruders had probably come in through the door leading to the patio in the back, which we usually left open when we were at home."

"Was anything stolen?" I asked.

He shook his head. "No, everything was still there—even her phone and all her jewelry. There was money in a jar on the kitchen counter that no one had touched. Nancy might have surprised them by being at the house, and they either killed her and took the body with them to get rid of, or they kidnapped her, maybe for trafficking. That's what we were told."

"And the children? They were teenagers at the time. Where were they?"

"They were with friends. It was a Friday night, and they were having sleepovers. Nancy had arranged for them to be out of the house because she wanted it to be a special night for us...a night for us alone."

"And that's why she cooked dinner and expected you to come

home earlier," I said. "Was your marriage in trouble?"

He looked up. "Excuse me?"

"Were you having problems and trying to solve them? Was that what the dinner was about?"

He shrugged. "Maybe. I don't know. I thought we were doing fine, but I guess when thinking back on it like I have done a lot over the past five years, yes. I guess we had drifted apart. Nancy had started modeling, and I wasn't too happy about that. I didn't think she needed to; it's not like we needed the extra money. But she wanted to, she said for her own sake. I guess she needed to feel pretty again. She was a model when we met. It made her feel young, she said. So, I agreed to it, but it made me miserable. My wife didn't have to work. That's why I worked so hard, so she wouldn't have to."

"But maybe she liked it," I said.

"I know. I should have been happy for her. She was quite successful. I just didn't...think it was necessary."

I nodded, then noted it on my pad. It wasn't unusual for a couple in their situation or stage of life to struggle in their marriage, but it was still worth noting.

"Did you ever wonder if she just walked out on you? If she chose to leave?" I said, looking up from my notepad. His eyes met mine, and he hesitated before responding.

"Every day," he said. "I wondered if she had staged it to look like she was taken. My wife had a penchant for drama. For a long time, I wondered if she'd just come back on her own once she was done with her little spectacle."

"But, she never did."

"Until now," he said. "Now, she's back, and I don't know what to think of it, to be honest."

"Dad!"

A young man came up toward Charles. Charles' face lit up at the sight of the boy who was very obviously his son. As they hugged, I saw a young woman who had to be his sister come up behind him. She hugged Charles as well. I knew both of them were away for college, and it had taken a while for them to get here.

"Is it really true?" the man asked.

His father nodded.

"She's back?" the girl said.

"Yes, yes, she is. She's sleep…"

Tears sprang to both of their eyes as their father spoke like the realization was just beginning to sink in.

"But…I don't understand," the girl said, her voice quivering. "How? How is she suddenly back…now? After all these years?"

Charles sighed and pulled her into a hug. "It's okay, sweetie. I don't understand it either. I don't understand anything right now, to be honest."

Chapter 11

"I DON'T GET IT. Where were you?"

Nancy lifted her glance and locked eyes with her daughter. Charles had brought them in, and now they were staring at one another, not really knowing what to say.

"I told you," her father said. "Mom doesn't remember anything."

Her daughter narrowed her eyes, biting her cheek. She didn't want to come close enough for Nancy to reach out and touch her.

"How does she not remember? How can you be gone for five years and not know where you've been? It makes no sense."

Nancy tried to smile. The look in her daughter's eyes was hurtful. "Tinkerbell, I..."

Her daughter winced at the sound of her old nickname. Nancy had called her that since she was two years old and dressed up as Tinkerbell every day for almost a year. Her daughter used to love being called that. It had later evolved to *Tinker* or just *Tinks*. Just like her brother had always been Bubba or just Bubs. It was what he had called himself once he started to talk, so they had adapted it.

"No one has called me that in five years," she said.

"We don't use that anymore," Charles said.

That brought tears to Nancy's eyes. She had missed out on so much of her children's lives. Five years had gone by, and now they were both so grown up. In this instant, she realized she knew absolutely nothing about them. So much could have changed in this time. What did they like to do? Who were their friends? Did they do any sports? Did Tinks still play the cello? Did Bubba still swim? All she knew was that they had both left for college, and that was why it took a while for them to get there once she showed up. It wasn't exactly the reunion she had hoped for or looked forward to while lying in the hospital bed, dreaming about them.

"I'm not sure, I can…to me, you'll always be Tinks," she said, tears rolling down her cheeks. Nancy reached out her hands toward her daughter, but she pulled away. "I'm sorry. I'm sorry for being away."

Bubba walked up to her, then put his hand in hers. His soft brown eyes locked with hers, and she could tell he was struggling to keep the tears back. He had always been the sensitive one. People said you couldn't love your children equally, but that wasn't how Nancy felt. She loved them the same amount. She just liked Bubba better because he was easier. He always had been easier.

"My sweet boy," Nancy said and kissed the top of his hand.

Bubba's body started to tremble as the tears overwhelmed him. He still tried to keep them back, resulting in his body almost convulsing. Nancy pulled his hand, and he came closer, but not enough for her to hug him.

Nancy let go of the boy, and he pulled back, hiding his face between his hands. Nancy looked at Tinkerbell, but she wasn't going to come any closer. Her arms remained crossed in front of her chest, and she stared at Nancy like she didn't even want to know about her. Only the occasionally sniffle revealed that she too was struggling to keep the tears back.

"Tinks, listen…" Nancy said, but the girl turned away, so she didn't even look at her.

"I'm going back to the house," she said, addressed to her dad. "I don't have anything to say to her."

"Tinkerbell, please…at least give me a chance to ex…"

She turned around and looked at her mother, eyes ablaze. "No. I don't want to hear it. I don't believe this act of yours. Not for even a second do I believe you can't remember anything."

That hit Nancy like a punch in the stomach. She could barely breathe as she watched her daughter rush out of the hospital room.

"She'll come around," Charles said, forcing a smile. "Just give her a little time."

Chapter 12

WE WAITED until the family had their reunion, then walked in and asked if we could talk again with Nancy. The tension in the room was so thick I could have cut it. The dad and the son were the only ones there, and they said goodbye to Nancy, then left.

"How did it go?" I asked and approached her. I hoped she'd be ready to talk some more, but she barely lifted her eyes to look at me.

"Not well, huh?"

"What do you want? I'm in a terrible mood."

"I just thought maybe we could talk some more about the night you disappeared and what you remember," I said.

She lifted her glare, and her eyes met mine. "Why? Why do you want to know?"

I narrowed my eyes, not quite understanding the question. "The sheriff has asked us to help investigate what really happened to you. I thought you'd want me to find out. Don't you want to know?"

I sat down on a chair, scrutinizing this woman. She was hard to read.

"I don't know," she said and reached out her hands. "I don't know what I want right now. Or maybe I do. I want to get back to be with my family, but they don't want me anymore. I've been replaced by some other woman, apparently, and my daughter won't even talk to me. Right now, I'm just trying to survive."

I nodded. "I understand. But we think it's very important to find out what happened, so it won't happen to someone else. Our job is to make sure that if someone hurt you, which we think someone did, then they're brought to justice."

Nancy's eyes landed on my stomach. "You're pregnant, aren't you?"

Instinctively, I looked down like I wanted to make sure I really was, then raised my eyes again with a nod.

"Yes."

Nancy exhaled. "Do me a favor and enjoy it. You don't know when you might lose it all. You might suddenly wake up, and then it's all gone. Cherish it while it lasts."

I cleared my throat. "I understand why you might feel that way, but..."

Tears sprang to Nancy's eyes as she interrupted me. "No, you don't. Don't patronize me. You don't understand anything that I'm going through right now. Don't pretend that you do."

That shut me up. She was so right. No one knew what it was like to be her at this moment.

"Even so...we need to know what happened, and I need you to..."

I had barely finished the sentence before Nancy turned her back on me and closed her eyes.

"Not now. I can't deal with this right now. You'll have to come back."

Matt gave me a look that meant he was ready to leave her alone. I agreed. She was dealing with a huge shock and needed to process that.

"We'll be back later, and then we'll talk," I said as I reached the door. Matt was holding it open for me. Just as I said the words, Nancy lifted her head and glared at me. The look in her eyes made me almost drop the notepad in my hand.

There was such great fear in them; it made me lose my breath.

Chapter 13

I WAS STARVING, so we stopped for a hot dog at a Seven-Eleven on the way back. My mom stayed with the kids, and I knew she had cooked, but the last thing I needed right now was some gluten-free, vegan dish. The baby demanded meat. At least that was my excuse.

We sat in my minivan, eating the hotdogs and washing them down with some unhealthy soda, which I had promised my mom I would stop drinking now that I was *responsible for more than myself.*

Matt took the last bite, then slurped his soda. I was so happy that he liked to eat junk like me, even if he was better at eating healthy in general than I was. It made me feel less guilty.

"So, what do you think?" he asked and wiped his greasy fingers on a napkin.

"About Nancy?"

He nodded and put down the soda. "Do you think she's telling the truth?"

"I don't know, to be honest," I said. "But why would she lie?"

"So, you think she really can't remember anything?"

I shrugged. "I have to admit it is strange and a little too convenient that she can't remember where she has been for the past five years, and yet she does remember her family and things from their childhood."

"But the doctor did say that the blow to her head has affected her short-term memory," Matt added. "That it wasn't unusual."

"But then again, what if you don't want to tell where you've been?" I said.

"You mean like she ran away with some guy, then decided to come back?" Matt asked. "I could go for that theory. But what about the morphine in her blood and the blow to her head, not to mention the bruises on her wrists?"

"He might have been a terrible choice in boyfriend," I said with a small chuckle. "No, I don't think that would be why she's decided to lie. If she is lying."

"Then, why would she?" Matt asked.

I touched my stomach and caressed it gently. "If you ask me, I can't imagine how any mother would just be able to leave her children and stay away for five years. I could never do that."

"But some moms do," Matt said, looking out the window.

I dug into the second hot dog that I had bought and told Matt not to comment on. "And the morphine and jumping in the water could have been her trying to commit suicide after realizing she had lost everything. That would be an explanation for the morphine and maybe the blow to the head that could have happened when falling in."

"But it doesn't explain the bruised wrists," I said, then paused while finishing the last hot dog and wiping ketchup off my fingers. I started up the minivan and looked at Matt. "Nor does it explain the deep fear in her eyes that I saw just before we left. If you ask me, I think she is withholding something from us, maybe even a lot. But I don't think she's hiding it because she doesn't want us to know where she's been. I think she's too scared to tell. That's my two cents on that; now, let's go home to the kids. I want to look at them and enjoy them while I still have them."

"She got to you after all, didn't she?" Matt said. "With what she said."

I drove the minivan into A1A and accelerated without answering him. I didn't want to admit to him that she had gotten to me big time. I couldn't stop thinking about how awful it had to be to come back after five years, and then your family had just moved on without you. It had to be crushing her heart. No matter if she was lying or not.

Chapter 14

THEN:

"That sure was some fine chicken."

Billy grabbed his plate and put it in the kitchen sink. Jade and her brother Ethan did the same. They helped clear off the table, and Billy did the dishes. After cleaning up, they all went to the living room and sat on the couches. Billy plopped down next to Jade. She rubbed her neck, and he noticed.

"Are you having problems with your neck?" he asked.

She removed her hand, feeling shy that he would notice. "It's nothing. I just woke up with a pain. It's annoyed me all day."

"I can help you with that," Billy said. "Do you want me to massage it? I'm known to have magical hands."

He lifted his hands in the air, then smiled. Jade blushed, then shook her head. Ethan looked up briefly from his phone, then returned to scrolling, probably reading one of his webtoons like he always did. Jade's brother was such a geek.

"It's okay," Jade said with a shy smile.

Billy leaned forward. "Are you sure? I'm actually really good at it. You probably just have a little muscle pain. Nothing a good rubbing can't cure."

Jade glanced at her mother, who approached them, bringing Billy another beer. She placed it on the table in front of him, then left to grab a new bottle of wine. She already had two glasses during dinner, Jade noticed. And now she was opening another bottle? On a school night?

"Did Dad call?" Jade asked, suddenly slightly uncomfortable.

Her mother pulled out the cork, then looked at her. "He's on the road. It'll probably be late before he gets to the hotel. We'll talk with him tomorrow."

Jade looked down at her phone, then opened her latest text from her father. She suddenly missed him terribly. She felt Billy's hand touch her neck gently.

"Boy, you're tense. Let me loosen those muscles for you, Jadie-girl."

Jadie-girl? What the heck was that? A nickname?

Jade pulled away, but Billy became insistent. His fingers grabbed around her neck and started to massage. It actually felt pretty amazing. Jade closed her eyes and let him do it while the tension she had felt all day subsided.

Billy smiled. "See? I told you I had magical fingers."

"It feels really nice," Jade said.

His fingers moved around on her skin, rubbing the sore spots, and Jade couldn't help herself. She enjoyed it.

"Why aren't you married, Billy?" she asked while his fingers massaged her, touching her skin gently, causing goosebumps to rise on her arms.

He glanced toward her mother with a soft smile. "It just wasn't really meant to be, I guess."

Billy let go of her neck, then looked at her. "There you go. Now you feel better, don't you?"

She nodded, blushing once again. Billy grinned and put his arm around her shoulder, then pulled her close until her head leaned on his chest. She could smell his cologne. It was sweet and a little nauseating.

Ethan lifted his eyes and stared at them. Then he shook his head, rose to his feet, and left. Seeing this, Jade pulled away from Billy, grabbed her phone, and texted her dad goodnight.

Chapter 15

AFTER THREE DAYS in the hospital, Nancy was released. Charles came to pick her up in his car and helped her get in. They drove to the south end of the island in deep silence. Nancy felt tears pile up in her eyes as they reached Old Settlement Road, and she saw the house towering in front of them. She swallowed hard in order not to cry.

Finally, she was home again. She couldn't wait to sleep in her own bed or to cook in her own kitchen again. Even though the kids had left the nest, there still needed to be food on the table.

Charles stopped the car in the driveway and killed the engine. She thought he'd get out, but he didn't. Instead, he sat with his hands on the wheel, holding it so hard his knuckles were turning white.

"Charles?" she asked. "What's going on?"

He shook his head. "I've made the bed in the guest cottage for you. You can stay there until you find somewhere else to live."

Nancy lowered her eyes and looked at her fingers. Her stomach was in knots, and she fought not to cry. "The guest cottage, but…this is my home, Charles. We're still married."

He shook his head. "Come on, Nancy. You seriously expect me to throw everything away? I am married to Tanya now. I can't just go back to the way things used to be. You can't ask that of me."

Nancy nodded, biting back tears. Of course, things wouldn't be the same again. How could she have been so stupid to think they would be?

"So, you're shoving me away. Hiding me in the back?"

Charles growled, annoyed. "That's not how it is. This is what we can do right now. Take it or leave it."

"I see," Nancy said and got out of the car. She stood for a few seconds and stared at the front door with the heart wreath she had bought many years ago and loved so dearly. It belonged to someone else now. She'd have to accept that.

"Luckily, I saved some of your old stuff that I never got around to throwing away," Charles said. "Clothes and such. I put it all in the guest cottage, so you'll at least have something to wear."

Nancy tried to smile. "Thank you. Appreciate it."

He stared at her, scrutinizing her, narrowing his eyes. "You really don't remember anything? Not even a little bit?"

Nancy shook her head with an exhale.

"I'll be in the guest cottage in case you need me, which I guess you won't. Thank you for letting me stay here. I have nowhere else to go."

Nancy walked into the yard, glancing cautiously at the big Victorian house that once had belonged to her, wondering how it had been so easy for them all to replace her. She spotted a figure in one of the windows and realized it had to be Tanya, Charles' new wife.

Her replacement.

Chapter 16

I DIDN'T MANAGE to get Nancy to talk to me much, even though I went to the hospital every day. On the third day, Detective Roberts from the sheriff's office called me.

"We've decided to drop the case. Sheriff's decision."

I sat down on my couch, pressing the phone against my ear. "Drop it? But we've barely begun?"

Roberts exhaled deeply at the other end. "I know. And I promised the sheriff to say we're sorry to have involved you, but there really isn't much more we can do at this point."

"What happened to *we need to find out what happened, so it won't happen to someone else? We need to figure out if a crime has been committed*?"

He exhaled again. I knew he wanted me just to give in, but I wasn't ready to. I believed there was something here, something that needed to be uncovered.

"I don't know, Thomas. But Mrs. Henry isn't exactly cooperating much. You've tried for days now to get some bits and pieces out of her, with no luck. She doesn't even seem interested in figuring out what happened to her. Her husband can't really help either, and we have no evidence to build a case upon. It's all just a lot of suspicions and innuendoes."

"What if I tell you I think she's hiding something?" I asked.

"It's not exactly a crime," he said.

"No, but what if she's lying to protect herself?" I asked. "If she's too scared to tell us the truth?"

"Has she given you any reason to believe that?" Roberts asked. "Has she said anything?"

"I see great fear in her eyes," I said.

Roberts sighed. "Not exactly hard evidence."

"I know, but it's enough for me to know that something more is going on here and that I am being lied to."

"But is that enough to use a bunch of resources on? Times are tough. We have to cut our spending. I am sorry, Eva Rae, but the decision has been made. We're closing the case for now. If something comes up, we'll reopen it, okay?"

Knowing there wasn't anything else I could do, I accepted it, then hung up, throwing my phone angrily on the couch.

Matt looked up from his computer. "I don't have to ask what that was all about. I guess we're out, then."

He closed the lid on his computer, then looked at me. "Uh-oh. I don't care for that look in your eyes, Eva Rae. Remember, you're pregnant. You need to rest. I think this is for the best for all of us."

I shook my head, biting my nails. "I'm not ready to give up yet. Something is wrong here, and I can't just leave it alone."

Matt gave me a look of disappointment. "There isn't more you can do, Eva Rae. Let it go, will you? Please?"

I couldn't promise him that, so instead, I just didn't say anything.

Chapter 17

THE SMALL KITCHEN in the guest cottage worked well enough for Nancy to cook herself a light meal. Charles had made sure to stock up the fridge and cabinets with just enough for her to get by for a few days. It was very thoughtful of him and made her shed a few tears as she stirred the pot with the tomato sauce. Charles had always been a good husband to her. She regretted so deeply that she hadn't been better at taking care of their marriage. There had been many fights before her disappearance. They had struggled.

And now it was all over. She had lost him. She had lost the house and the children who barely knew her anymore.

I used to have everything. Now, I have nothing.

Nancy sat down and ate her pasta dish while looking out the big windows toward the house. There had been a time when she had hated that place. She had felt trapped there when the children were young. She had blamed Charles for forcing her to give up her career as a model. Charles had never liked that world and wanted to save her from it. But Nancy had loved it and begged him to allow her to return to it. There was a photographer, Miles, who had called her repeatedly and said he had a job for her that she was absolutely perfect for. She had told him she couldn't—that now she was a housewife and had lost her looks, but he didn't believe her. In the end, he had come to her door, and as she opened it, he had told her she was every bit as stunning as she had been when younger, maybe even more so since now she had a depth to her look, a maturity that the world of fashion was craving these days.

She had fallen for his flattery and accepted the job. Excited, she had told Charles about it, but he got angry.

"There's no need for you to work," he said. "Don't you have everything you want? Plus, the kids need you at home."

She had argued that they were in school all day anyway, and she could easily make it back in time to pick them up. Then she had begged him and told him how much it meant to her. But he wouldn't hear of it.

She did it anyway. Charles was infuriated once she told him, but by then, it was too late. She had believed he would come around once he saw the results, but he refused to even look at the magazine once she wanted to show it to him.

He felt betrayed, he said. And something broke between them after that. He looked at her differently, and Nancy didn't feel comfortable. She felt dirty. Like he somehow believed what she had done was disgusting. Charles didn't like his woman to be dressed up like a doll and shown off in some magazine where others would be looking at her. To him, she was selling her body and was no better than a stripper. Even if it was a fancier version of one, she was no better.

Nancy finished her pasta dish and grabbed her plate to wash it off in the sink when the phone on the counter lit up. Charles had been so kind as to leave a phone in the cottage for her. He had told her she could keep it until she got back on her feet.

Nancy grabbed it and looked at the display, reading a text she had received. It read:

YOU SHOULDN'T HAVE COME BACK

Chapter 18

OLD SETTLEMENT ROAD was one of the most exclusive neighborhoods on Merritt Island. It was a closed road with only a few big houses flanked on each side and lots of flourishing Florida landscape, including tall trees with Spanish moss dangling from their branches. The Henrys' house had water views, and their own boat dock out to the Indian River. It also had a huge pool area overlooking the river and was gorgeous in every way possible. It was painted in a light pink color that made me think of my daughters' three-story dollhouse when they were younger.

"What are we doing here, Mom?" Christine said from the seat next to me. "I thought you were taking me to the mall?"

"I will be in a minute," I said and stopped the minivan in front of the Henrys' mansion. "I just need to do something first."

"I'm gonna be late. Clarissa and Brooke won't wait for me if I'm late, Mom."

"Of course, they will. If you agreed to meet up, they'll wait for you. Don't be silly."

"No, they won't," she groaned. "They'll ditch me."

"I'll only be a minute."

"No, you won't. You'll start talking to these people, and then I'll be late."

My thirteen-year-old sighed deeply and returned to her phone.

I ignored her and got out. I knew I had sort of promised to leave this case alone, but I had been awake all night, thinking about Nancy, worrying that she was in danger but just wouldn't tell us. There was so much I didn't understand about her story. I went through the old case files from when she disappeared and couldn't make sense of it. There had been blood on one of the floors in the living room, Nancy's blood. She had been hurt. And then she had disappeared. The neighbors hadn't seen anything, according to the report. I found that so hard to believe in a neighborhood like this. It was so quiet here; all you could hear were the cicadas and the water lapping against the rocks.

I stared at the front entrance of their house. The theory was that someone had come in through the back door, attacked Nancy, and maybe kidnapped her. It had all taken place before ten-thirty in the evening when Charles came home. Most people living here were families with children or older people. They were all at home that night, according to the report. The only one who wasn't was an old couple who lived at the end of the street. They had been out of town, visiting with their children and grandchildren. But the rest? They hadn't heard a thing.

How was that possible?

They fought a lot, was one explanation. It wasn't unusual to hear a commotion from the Henrys' house. Nancy and Charles weren't doing so well in their marriage, one neighbor, Mrs. Berkeley, had said. She believed they might have been heading for a divorce. She lived across the street, but according to the report, she had been passed out drunk the night it happened. She had slept through the whole thing.

How convenient.

I walked up to the house, approaching the front door, when I spotted Nancy in the yard, sitting outside what appeared to be a guest cottage with a cup of coffee on the small table in front of her.

Chapter 19

"NOTHING BEATS THE QUIETNESS HERE, HUH?"

Nancy looked up at me, then turned her head away. "What do you want?"

I noticed she was fumbling nervously with a phone between her fingers. She kept looking at it, then put it on the table in front of her. When she put it down, she was tapping her fingers on her thighs.

"I came to talk to you," I said. "I thought maybe you were ready to talk now that you were out of the hospital?"

She scoffed. "You think I suddenly remember everything just because I was released?"

"I thought maybe coming home would help jolt your memory, yes. Are you staying in the guest cottage?"

She grabbed her coffee and sipped it.

"I get it," I said. "He lives there with his new wife, right?"

She exhaled, her eyes lingering on the table in front of her.

"Have you been inside yet? Or are there too many bad memories?"

"I'm not going inside," Nancy said. "*She* lives there now. It's her house. She's married to him now."

"I'm not sure that would hold up in court," I said.

Nancy looked up at me. "You don't think so?"

"Technically, you were married to him first, and you were never divorced. Half of that house ought to belong to you."

Nancy stared at the water, then shook her head. "I'm not sure… I'm beginning to think they were all better off without me coming back here."

I bit my lip. "You're scared, am I right? I see it in your eyes."

Nancy shook her head. It wasn't convincing.

"What are you keeping from me, Nancy?" I asked. "If anyone has hurt you, we need to find them and bring them to justice before they hurt someone else. Don't you see that?"

She lowered her head and looked at her feet below. When she spoke, it was with barely a whisper.

"Please, just go."

"Nancy, I am here for you. I worry that whoever harmed you will do so again. To be honest, I fear you are in great danger."

Nancy glanced briefly at the phone in front of her, and I saw something change in her face like she contemplated for just a second whether she should tell me everything. But then it was gone.

"I'll be fine."

I stared at the phone, then at her, and noticed her hands were shaking heavily. "Someone is threatening you. That's why you won't talk to me."

Nancy closed her eyes. Her tone was flat and distant, yet I could hear a small quiver in her voice as she spoke:

"Please, just leave me alone. Please."

Chapter 20

CHRISTINE WAS LITERALLY SCREAMING at me as I rushed toward the Merritt Island Square Mall. We were way too late, and I had promised her we wouldn't be. I was so selfish. I didn't argue with her, just ignored her and drove up by the entrance to the courtyard and stopped.

"Why do you always have to ruin everything?" was the last thing she asked me before she left the car, slamming the door behind her.

I watched her enter the mall fifteen minutes later than she had promised her friends. I just hoped they hadn't ditched her. She'd never forgive me. I felt bad. But then again, it didn't matter what I did these days. Everything was wrong; even the way I breathed would be commented on from time to time. I was in for a couple of tough years with this one. Luckily, Olivia had gotten easier over the past few months and eased up on me. But, boy, I was tired of repeatedly being told what was wrong with me and being involved in all the drama with their friends.

A wave of nausea overwhelmed me as I left the parking lot, and I reached out for my bag of Krispy Kreme donuts that I had bought at the gas station on my way there. It wasn't exactly healthy, and I was glad Matt wasn't here, but it was what the baby craved. At least that's what I told myself. The nausea subsided as my stomach was filled, and I felt satisfied again. It had been the same through all my pregnancies. I got nausea from hunger.

This morning, Matt had gone back to the station to work on another case that Annie assigned him. Meanwhile, I had nothing much else to do other than obsessing about Nancy Henry and her strange story. I knew she wanted me to leave it alone; heck, everyone wanted me to do that. But I couldn't. I simply couldn't get myself to do it.

Washing down the donut with the rest of my coffee that had gone cold, I drove back down to South Merritt Island. I was supposed to pick up Christine in two hours anyway. It would be a waste of time to go all the way back to Cocoa Beach. I would barely make it home before I had to leave again. It was Saturday, and Olivia had promised to look after Alex. She had a big project to do in French, so she wasn't planning on going anywhere anyway.

I had time.

I drove back down South Tropical Trail and found Old Settlement Road once again. It was such a quaint little area, and you could easily miss the road if you didn't know it was there. A small Georgianna wooden church that looked like it was taken out of an old southern movie lay decoratively at the beginning of the street between the tall trees and the dangling Spanish moss. A woman was putting out flowers on the porch by the entrance as I drove past it. She looked up at my car, and I gave her a casual wave like you did in neighborhoods like these.

She waved back.

I stopped in front of the Henrys' house again but then took a turn left and drove up in front of the house across the street from them.

I got out and walked up to the front porch, opened the screen, and knocked.

Berkeley, it said in gold letters on the door.

Chapter 21

"YES?"

I showed the woman in the door my badge and told her my name. She squinted her eyes and came so close that I could smell the alcohol on her breath.

"I'd like to ask you a couple of questions. Can I come in?"

The woman hesitated, then stepped aside so I could walk past her. She closed the door behind me, and I walked into the dark living room. The air was musty and stale, even though the AC was running. We sat down on her leather couches. They had once been very nice and looked expensive, but now they were worn out.

"It's about them, isn't it?" she asked and nodded toward the Henrys' house across the street.

I nodded. "Yes."

"Is it really true?" Mrs. Berkeley asked. "That she is back?"

I nodded again. "Yes. She is back, and that's why we have reopened the case of her disappearance from back then."

It wasn't exactly the entire truth, but she didn't have to know that.

"We're trying to figure out what happened to her."

Mrs. Berkeley glanced to the side, and I noticed she was staring at a bottle of brandy on a side table. I wondered if she was craving a glass. It wouldn't surprise me.

"Now, I found your testimony from back then," I said.

"I told them everything," she said. "I was drunk. I'm not proud to say it, but I didn't see or hear anything since I had been drinking heavily that night. I had lost my husband only a few months earlier, so I was a mess."

"I understand," I said.

"Then you'll also understand that I can't be of much help. Even if I did see something, my testimony wouldn't hold up in court. I'm not what you'd call a reliable witness."

I looked up, and my eyes met Mrs. Berkeley's. "But you did see something, didn't you? I mean, you can hardly have avoided it."

Mrs. Berkeley rubbed her hands against one another as they were getting clammy. It was a sure sign I was onto something.

"What didn't you tell them, Mrs. Berkeley? Now is the time to get it off your chest. As you said yourself, it probably won't hold up in court, but maybe it can help direct my investigation."

"I don't know; I'm not…"

"Please, Mrs. Berkeley. Something happened to Nancy Henry that night, and now that she is back, I fear for her life. If you know something, anything, then you need to tell me. I fear for her life the way it is now."

I placed my hand on her arm and looked into her eyes to make sure she understood the importance of this.

Mrs. Berkeley took a deep breath. "There was something I never said to anyone."

"Yes?"

She swallowed and exhaled. "But you don't have it from me, do you hear? I will deny it if anyone asks."

Chapter 22

"I HEARD THEM FIGHTING. It went on for about an hour or so. Lots of yelling and screaming at one another." Mrs. Berkeley's hands were shaking as she spoke to me. She saw me staring at them and hid them in her lap.

"There was a lot of that going on before her disappearance—them yelling at one another, but this night it was different."

"How so?"

"It was louder. More violent."

"Did you see anything?"

Mrs. Berkeley nodded pensively. "I saw Nancy leave the house at one point. She ran out from the garage, but then a shadow came up behind her and pulled her back in."

"So, she was pulled back in the house against her will?"

"Yes."

"Did you see who the person was?"

Mrs. Berkeley shook her head. "It was dark. I couldn't see a face."

"Could it have been Charles? Her husband?"

Mrs. Berkeley looked down. I nodded. "That's what you fear it was, right? You were scared it was him, and that's why you didn't tell the police. Because he might come after you, and now by talking to me, you fear he'll find out."

Mrs. Berkeley looked up again. "I was scared to death when I saw her be pulled back like that. I didn't dare tell anyone."

"But do you think it was Charles you saw?"

"I couldn't see him properly, but he was about the same size. At the time, I was sure it was him, but as the years have passed, I started doubting it. Charles is such a nice man. I couldn't see how he would harm his own wife."

"Some men do," I said. "Even nice ones."

Mrs. Berkeley nodded. "It has tormented me for years. I have been so worried about Nancy, and to be honest, I was certain she was dead. That someone killed her that night. Especially after..."

"After what?"

She cleared her throat. "That's the thing. It kept bothering me when I read the articles afterward or watched it on the news."

"What bothered you?"

"They never spoke about it, and so I started to wonder if I had dreamt it or hallucinated it while drinking."

I wrinkled my forehead. "Dreamt what? Mrs. Berkeley?"

She exhaled and glanced at the bottle once again. "I'm gonna be in trouble when I tell you this."

"Please, just tell me anyway."

She bit her lip, then nodded, sweat springing to her upper lip.

"Here's the deal. That night, I heard more than yelling and screaming. There was something else too. I have kept it with me for years, but I have to get it off my chest. It's weighing me down."

Chapter 23

MATT WAS at the house when I got back. He was sitting in the living room, his laptop on his knees, and looked up as Christine and I entered.

"Hi, Christine," Matt said, but she didn't answer. She scoffed, then rushed up the stairs, taking angry steps all the way to let me know how upset she was. I opened my mouth to yell at her to be nicer to Matt and at least say hello, then decided maybe this wasn't the time to lecture her. I could deal with it later when she had calmed down slightly, and I could actually talk to her.

Matt lifted his eyebrows. I bent down to kiss him. Elijah was with him, sitting in a recliner, playing a game on his iPad, wearing a big headset. They were both still living in Matt's small townhouse, and we hadn't really discussed what to do once the baby came along. I was kind of waiting for Matt to open the conversation. We had lived together before but not exactly successfully. I wasn't sure he wanted to try again.

On the other hand, this time, it was different. Now, we had a baby coming. I would want him to be around all day and night. Plus, we were a couple. We should live together, right? But then there was the problem of space. If they were to live with us, it would get quite crowded in my small house. My mom might have to find a place of her own. I wasn't ready to make that decision yet. I had grown to enjoy having her close, even though we fought a lot, and she always gave me those judgmental looks. I didn't like the thought of her living somewhere on her own, all alone.

"What's with Christine?" Matt asked.

I shook my head. "She's angry because I was late to pick her up at the mall. Her friends had already left, and she was all alone. The usual stuff. I can't do anything right. She should be happy I spent the entire day driving her, but no."

I threw myself on the couch next to Matt with a deep exhale, then kicked off my flipflops and massaged my swollen feet. I was sweating heavily and panting. Florida was a hot place to be pregnant.

"So, where were you?" he asked, giving me a suspicious look. "If you weren't at the mall. You didn't…no, Eva Rae."

"Yes, Matt. I went to talk to Nancy. She's out of the hospital, and I figured that maybe she would finally be able to talk."

"Let me guess, she didn't."

I shook my head. "Nope. But someone else did. And it was quite interesting what she told me."

Matt sat up straight on the couch. "Who?"

"The neighbor across the street. Mrs. Berkeley."

"But she was passed out drunk? Wasn't that what the report said?" Matt asked.

I shook my head. "She hadn't been drinking that night when it happened. She was actually trying to cut down on the alcohol. When she saw what happened across the street, she went straight back to the bottle. But she saw something first. Something that blows this story wide open and tells me that a crime was committed that night."

"Okay. Now, you have me intrigued," he said. "What did she see?"

I glanced toward Elijah to make sure he wasn't listening in on our conversation. He seemed occupied with his game and was wearing a headset.

"First of all, she heard them fight. She thought that they were just quarreling like they had a lot before. They weren't doing very well, she said, and many on the street guessed that they were up for a divorce soon. So, at first, she didn't react much to it, but then it got more violent and louder than usual, so she peeked out just in time."

"In time for what?"

"To see Nancy storm out of the garage, rushing out like she was running for her life. But a shadow came up behind her and grabbed her from behind, then pulled her back in the house."

"Really?"

I nodded.

"And who was it? Charles?"

"That's what we don't know. Mrs. Berkeley couldn't tell. He was about the same size, she said. But there's something else."

"Yes?"

"After Nancy was pulled back into the house, she heard a shot being fired. And then everything went quiet. That's when she grabbed the bottle and started to drink heavily to erase what she had seen and heard. Mrs. Berkeley was certain that Charles had killed Nancy since she was gone the next day, and the police were on her doorstep asking all these questions. At first, she wasn't sure she really had seen and heard what she did. She doubted it and thought maybe she had just been so drunk she had dreamt it, but the more time passed, the more she became certain that Charles had killed Nancy and gotten rid of the body. Every day since, she has thought about going to the police. But she was scared of Charles. She knew her testimony wouldn't hold up in a courtroom, and since Charles would be able to afford the best lawyers, she feared he'd go free if all they had was the testimony of a drunkard. And then she feared what he might do to her. She kept telling herself that it didn't matter. Her telling the police wouldn't bring Nancy back."

"So, let me get this straight. There was a fight, Nancy tried to run away but was pulled back inside the house, and then someone was shot that night in the Henrys' house," Matt said. "Or at least shot at. And then Nancy disappeared."

"Yes. Unfortunately, Mrs. Berkeley got so drunk that she didn't see anything else. But my question is, why didn't any other neighbor hear the shot?"

"Maybe they did but didn't want to get involved," Matt said. "Maybe they too were scared."

"Okay, but then another question is raised. Nothing in the tech's report indicates that there had been shots fired. No gun powder residue found, no bullet holes in the wall if the shot missed. There were no signs of a gun going off that night. How do you explain that?"

Matt thought it over. "I guess someone cleaned up after themselves."

"Exactly. But you can't clean up a bullet hole in a wall in just a few hours. I'd say that bullet didn't miss its target."

"So out there somewhere is a person with a wound from a bullet?" Matt said. "Could it have been Nancy? Could Charles have shot her and believed she was dead?"

"And then gotten rid of her body?" I asked. "Not knowing that she wasn't dead yet?"

"Maybe."

I nodded. It was plausible. "But where has she been the past five years then?"

"Good question," Matt said. "Hiding maybe? Fearing he might find her? And then she fell in the creek, hit her head, and forgot everything?"

"Sounds a little far-fetched, but it's a theory. Just how did she survive? If she were shot, she would have needed medical help."

"We could check the hospitals and see if they reported a patient coming in with a bullet wound that night."

"That sounds like a g…"

I didn't get to finish the sentence before my phone vibrated. It said Roberts on the display. This was a surprise.

"You're not gonna believe this, Thomas," he said, sounding out of breath. "I need you to come to Crooked Mile Road. Asap."

Chapter 24

THEN:

Her parents were hosting a barbecue for their neighbors and friends. Billy was invited too, and Jade watched him when he stood by the grill, talking to her dad, a beer clutched in his hand. Billy said something that made Jade's father laugh, and they clinked their beer bottles before drinking. As Billy lifted the bottle to his lips, he glanced toward Jade, who was standing on the back porch. As their eyes locked, Jade felt her heart drop. She knew she was blushing. She always did when he was nearby. She didn't understand why. It was out of her control. As the bottle left his lips, his eyes were still locked with hers, and he smiled secretively.

Jade lowered her eyes shyly and suddenly became very aware that her dress showed too much cleavage for her liking. Her breasts looked like they could pop out over the edge at any time. And it was way too short for her liking. Embarrassed by this, Jade turned around, then walked back inside.

"There you are," her mother said. She was holding a dish with raw meat in her hands. "Could you take this out to your father?"

Jade stared at the steaks and hotdogs. She knew she'd have to take it out to them, to her dad and Billy, who was with him. She suddenly felt awful. She shook her head, then rushed up the stairs while her mother yelled something after her.

Jade hid in the bathroom while she could hear more guests arriving downstairs and her mother greeting them with that over-joyous voice that was nothing but a façade, hiding the fact that she was continually crying in her bedroom when no one was looking. Jade felt profound nausea overwhelm her when thinking about Billy and how he had looked at her, his eyes undressing her. She felt so dirty and decided to take a shower to wash off the sensation.

No one would miss her anyway. And she had no one to talk to. Her geeky brother and his friends were playing computer games in his room, and the grown-ups were busy drinking and chatting about ridiculous stuff like the weather or taxes—stuff that didn't interest her one bit.

While the water rushed down her body, washing all the bad feelings away, Jade decided she wouldn't go back down. She didn't want to be a part of it anyway. It was her parents' party, not hers. She would put on her PJs and watch TV in her room instead. Her mom could bring her food later on, or she could sneak down to the kitchen and grab some. She wasn't that hungry anyway.

The thought of hiding out in her room made her feel better. She had thought she wanted to dress up and be a part of the barbeque like she used to when younger. But not anymore. Being down there made her feel uncomfortable in a way she hadn't experienced before.

Jade turned off the shower, then wrapped herself in a towel and walked out to the hallway, going back to her room.

"Jade? Hey, sweetie."

Jade froze. Her hand holding the towel began to shake as Billy approached her, coming up the stairs.

"Where did you go?"

She turned to face him, heart pounding in her chest. Billy smiled gently. "You just disappeared. Aren't you coming back? Why did you take off that dress? You looked so pretty in it."

Again, Jade could feel herself blushing. She lowered her eyes so she wouldn't have to look into his. "I just…I needed a shower. I don't really want to go back down there. I…there really isn't anything for me down there."

"It's just boring grow-ups, huh? Well, to tell you the truth, they bore me as well from time to time. Well, most of the time."

"Really?"

"Are you kidding me? I hate that stuff—talking about tax deductions or dropping house prices. Nothing could be more boring, in my opinion. I almost didn't come tonight because I knew it would be like that. Yet, I am glad that I did. And it means a lot to your parents that I am here. But I have to say that you really looked like a grown woman out there, standing on the porch in that dress. If I didn't know better, I'd guess you were twenty."

That made Jade smile. She knew she looked older than most of her friends, but she had never heard anyone say it.

"I'm only sixteen," she said.

"I know, you silly," he said and came closer. "I was there for your birthday, remember?"

She did remember. Jade's dad had been out of town on her birthday, so her mom had asked Billy to come over for cake. Billy had been so sweet and bought her a leather jacket, the one she wanted the most, the one her mother wouldn't give her because she was way too young to wear something like that. But, apparently, Billy didn't think she was too young.

"How's your neck? Is it still bothering you?" he asked. "You look a little stiff."

He came even closer and reached out his hand to touch her neck, but she pulled away. He stopped her and gave her an intense look.

"Just let me feel it, okay?"

She let him, and his fingers moved across her neck, massaging her gently. "You're very tense, girl. You need to relax a little."

She pulled away, and his hand slid back, then landed on her shoulder. His finger continued massaging her. "Your shoulders are hard as rocks. Do you want me to rub them for you?"

She shook her head. "It's okay. I'm fine."

She felt warm and was suddenly very aware that she was naked underneath just a towel.

"I can give you a real massage if you want to," he continued. "I promise you'll like it. You'll like it so much that you'll come asking for more afterward."

Chapter 25

ROBERTS SPOTTED my minivan as I drove up the driveway. The house on Crooked Mile Road in Merritt Island was no more than an old wooden shack. The porch was overgrown with plants, and a tree had fallen onto the side of it, destroying parts of the roof. The yard was almost impassable due to the wilderness growing there, telling me no one had lived on this property for many years.

"Eva Rae, boy, am I glad to see you."

"What's going on?"

Matt had stayed behind to be with the kids when I left. He wasn't happy that I got called out to this and was about to protest when I told him I had to go.

"You're pregnant. You don't have to do anything except rest and eat. I'm scared you're risking the health of our child," was his argument.

He said it even though he knew it was completely lost on me.

It was dark out, and I could only see parts of the property when the light from the deputies' flashlights fell on the trees and lit up the area.

"I need you to come with me to the back," Roberts said and started walking. I followed him through the bushes and into the high grass. I was happy that I had decided to wear sneakers instead of flipflops.

"We were alerted to this place by an anonymous call that arrived late tonight. The caller said he was a neighbor and thought we should take a look at the place. It has been abandoned for ten years. The owner couldn't pay the bills and left. It belongs to the bank now."

Roberts escorted me through the yard until we reached a small shed in the back. The techs in their bodysuits were taking pictures.

I peeked inside, then felt my heart drop.

"What is this place?"

I stepped inside, careful where I set my feet, then knelt next to a set of shackles chained to the wall. I looked up at Roberts.

"Naturally, the first person we thought of was Nancy Henry," he said.

I nodded and looked around me. A small bowl of water in the corner had flies and dirt in it. There was only a little water on the bottom. Another bowl next to it was empty.

"So, you're saying you think this is where she was kept?" I asked with a shiver. The very thought was terrifying. Had Nancy been a prisoner there? If so, for how long? The entire five years? It didn't seem possible that anyone would survive that. Nancy had been slightly underweight and dehydrated when she was admitted; I just remembered that the doctor had told us. "You think that she has been eating and drinking out of those bowls? Like an animal?"

He nodded. "We found hairs on the floorboards. We're taking samples and will have them analyzed for DNA. My bet is it'll be a fit with Nancy."

"We need to bring her here," I said, looking around, then moving out of the way so the techs could do their work. "It might help jolt her memory, being here again."

Roberts smiled. "Way ahead of you. I had a patrol car pick her up earlier. She's still sitting in the back seat in the driveway. I wanted you to be here when she saw it. If she was kept here, then we'll need to reopen the case."

"I'll go get her," I said and rushed out of the small shed, the smell of decay still lingering in my nostrils. As I walked toward the patrol car, I kept wondering how on earth Nancy would have survived five years in this shed, even if she was fed and had enough water to drink. Being inside that place during a Florida summer had to be torture. Who on this earth would hate Nancy so intensely that they'd do this to her?

Chapter 26

"WHAT IS THIS PLACE? I really don't like it here."

I had asked Nancy to follow me down the yard, and she was doing so, even though it was very reluctantly.

"Do you recognize anything?" I asked while we walked.

She turned to look at me. It was dark out now, as the sun had set completely, but the techs had put up lamps to light up the entire yard, so they could work. One of them lit up her face as she stared at me, her eyes pensive.

"I...don't know."

"Maybe if we go over here," I said and guided her toward the shed. We turned around the old wooden house and through the thick, lush bushes. I held the branches to the side for Nancy so she could get past them.

Then she stopped abruptly.

"What is it? Nancy? Do you recognize anything here?" I asked. I walked up to her side, then placed a hand on her shoulder. She stood like she was frozen, her body completely stiff.

"W...what is this place?"

"Do you recognize it? Have you been here before?" I asked.

Roberts spotted us and came up toward us. I signaled for him not to disturb Nancy. I was hoping that seeing this place was jolting her memory. Anything would work at this point. If any little piece of her memory would come back, it might help us move forward.

"Nancy?"

She put a hand to her chest, and I could tell she was struggling to breathe properly. Her face went pale.

"Nancy? Are you okay?"

She didn't answer. Instead, she took a step forward toward the shed. The techs moved aside, directed by Roberts. Nancy grabbed the sides of the shed, then stepped in. I held my breath. I came up behind her and watched as she stood inside the shed, staring down at the chains and shackles that looked like they had been taken out of some awful horror movie. She glanced toward the two bowls, then clasped her mouth with a whimper. Her breathing grew shallower and faster, her chest heaving rapidly.

"Oh, God."

"Nancy? Are you okay?"

"It's…it's spinning," she said. "I can't…I…I…"

Nancy began to tilt. I ran toward her and grabbed her just as she was about to fall. Roberts came in behind me.

"Quick. We need her out of here. She's hyperventilating."

We lifted her and carried her outside, where we placed her carefully in the high grass. Someone brought her a bottle of water, and she sat up to drink, her eyes closed, still breathing raggedly.

I knelt next to her. "Are you okay, Nancy? You scared us in there."

She opened her eyes and looked at me. I saw something in them once again, the fear I had seen earlier at the hospital was back, and it was somehow deeper and even more chilling than earlier.

"I'm sorry. I just felt really bad in there."

"Nancy, I need you to talk to me a little here. Have you been in that shed before?"

Her eyes grew distant again. "I…I…those shackles…the bowl of water…"

"Yes? Did you recognize them?"

"I…I don't know."

"Nancy. Could this be the place you were kept after you were kidnapped five years ago? You have the bruises on your wrists. Did someone keep you here against your will?"

Her nostrils were flaring, her eyes flickering back and forth. She shook her head lightly. "I…I…"

She stopped, then looked up at me, her eyes wide. "I do remember being here. I have been inside of that shed before."

"Were you kept here? Nancy, this is important. Were you kept in that shed?"

She glanced down at her hands and wrists. The bruises were still very visible, the wounds where something had gnawed into the skin still apparent.

Then she nodded, tears spilling onto her hands.

Chapter 27

NANCY DIDN'T FEEL WELL when she was dropped off at the house by the FBI agent. Her hands were still shaking, and her heart was beating fast. Still, she had told them she wanted to go home. They had asked her a thousand questions, most of which she had no answer to. She wished she could describe everything in more detail, but she couldn't, she told them. She simply didn't remember.

"A good night's rest might help jolt your memory," Agent Eva Rae Thomas said as she helped her out of the car. "We'll talk again tomorrow. Maybe you'll remember more once you've slept on it. It might come back to you gradually in the coming days. It might get overwhelming. I wish there were someone who could stay with you tonight. I don't like that you're sleeping alone."

Nancy sent her a forced smile in the hope she would find it reassuring. "I'll be fine. I am used to solitude."

That made the FBI agent clam up. Her eyes grew big, and it almost looked like she would cry.

"I'm sorry," she said and used her hands as fans. "I just get really emotional these days."

"It's just the hormones," Nancy said.

"Yeah, I know. And you're right. But it just makes me so angry that anyone would do something like this to you. I can't…I'm sorry."

Nancy glanced at the big house that used to be hers. She wondered for a second if her children were still around or if they had gone back to their college dorms. She had wished she'd get to see them again before they did. She had hoped they'd be there when she got back from the hospital.

Maybe they're better off without you.

Nancy shook the thought. How could they be better off without their mother? No, they just needed time; that was all. They'd get used to the idea of her being around again. They'd get to know her again.

Somehow.

"I would like to go back now," Nancy said.

"Of course. Let me know if you need anything," Eva Rae Thomas said. "And if you remember anything, call me. I gave you my number, right?"

"Yes, you did."

"So, call me if you remember anything, even the smallest thing. You might think it's worthless and doesn't matter, but let me be the judge of that. You can call me anytime. I'll leave the phone on tonight, so you can call me in the middle of the night if you need to."

Nancy looked at the woman in front of her, then nodded. "All right. I appreciate it. I really do."

"Okay," Eva Rae said, then added right before she got into her minivan with all the toys filling the floor: "Anytime."

"I got it the first time," Nancy said and watched as she took off, waving eagerly out the window. There was something really sweet and innocent about this woman, and Nancy had to admit she was growing on her.

Nancy walked past the house and down toward the guest cottage while looking at the windows. There were lights in several of them, and she wondered if Charles and Tanya were having a great evening together, and if so, what were they doing? Watching TV? Reading?

Charles and Nancy had both loved reading, and before the kids came along, they had read to one another every night.

It had been her favorite thing to do together. Why had they stopped? Just because of the kids?

If only she could go back. That would be the first thing she'd do differently. She wouldn't stop doing the things she loved so much because of the children. She wouldn't have stopped being who she was just because of them.

Nancy shook her head, then walked up to the front of the guest cottage when she saw someone standing on the small porch outside, a tall shadowy figure.

"Why did you come back?" the voice behind the shadow asked.

Nancy felt her heart begin to race in her chest.

"What do you want?"

"Why are you here? Why didn't you just stay away?"

Nancy threw out her arms. "I don't know what you're talking about."

The shadow lifted something, and as the sparse light from the back porch of the big house fell on it, Nancy realized it was a gun. She stepped back, feeling her throat closing up.

"Please."

The gun was shaking in the hands of the holder. Nancy stepped back, reaching her hands up in front of her.

"Please, don't hurt me."

"No one wants you here," the voice said. "Don't you understand? Everyone thought you were dead."

"But I'm not," Nancy said, her voice quivering in fear.

The shadow didn't move. There was a long pause where Nancy wondered if the shadow had left. Then it said, the tone loaded with horrid vile:

"Not yet."

As the gun went off, Nancy threw herself to the grass and covered her head, screaming at the top of her lungs. It felt like an eternity went by, and she just laid there, shaking with fear. When she finally dared to lift her head, the shadow had gone.

Realizing this, Nancy rose to her feet, then ran panting and stumbling into the guest cottage. She locked the door behind her, then slid to the floor, her back against the door, hiding her face in her trembling hands.

When she was done crying, she pulled out her phone and found the FBI agent's number.

"You said anytime."

"Yes, of course, what's going on, Nancy?"

"My husband just tried to kill me; oh, Eva Rae, I am so scared. Please, help me."

Part II

TWO WEEKS LATER

Chapter 28

SHE SHOULDN'T BE DRINKING. Mrs. Berkley stared at the bottle in her hand. It was shaking heavily. She had promised not to, but it was just so hard when every fiber of her body craved it.

"Just one little drop," she mumbled. "No one will have to know."

No! You can't! It'll ruin everything. You promised.

She closed her eyes and bit the inside of her cheek. It was true. She had promised that FBI agent that she wouldn't drink anymore. They needed her sober so that no one could discredit her testimony.

Mrs. Berkeley took a deep breath and gathered herself...regained her composure. Of course, she could do this. She was stronger than this. She put the bottle down and walked away from it, turning her back on it.

"Maybe a cup of coffee instead," she told herself.

She had been doing so well until this morning. She had thrown all the bottles out and not touched a drop for two weeks. But this morning, she had found one she had stashed away in a cabinet upstairs; one she had entirely forgotten that she had stuck in between the towels. It had taken all her strength not to drink from it.

"Yes, coffee would do me good," she said, then walked into the kitchen and started the coffee maker she had gotten from her niece for Christmas last year. It could make all sorts of coffee and even grind the beans and everything, even though Mrs. Berkeley always only asked it to make just a black one. She never really used all the other features that her niece and her husband had told her about excitedly. Mrs. Berkeley didn't drink cappuccino or frappuccinos or whatever they were called. She didn't like milk in her coffee, so she didn't need a latte either. All she wanted was just plain, regular black coffee, so that was what she got.

The smell of it hit her face as the machine spat it out. It had a hint of hazelnut to it, not that Mrs. Berkeley cared much for that. She didn't understand why coffee couldn't just be that anymore. Why did it all have to have hazelnut or pumpkin spice taste? What was the point?

She did see the point of making it Irish, however, but she wasn't allowed to.

Mrs. Berkeley sat down at the kitchen table, cup in front of her, and today's *Florida Today* edition on the table. On the front cover was a picture of her former neighbor across the street, Nancy Henry.

Mrs. Berkeley felt her heart beat faster in her chest and breathed to calm herself. She fought the urge to run into the living room and grab the bottle.

"It'll be over soon, Maria," she whispered to herself. "It'll soon be all over, and then you can go back to living your life the way you want to. You won't have to be afraid anymore."

It was pure luck that she had been sober on the night that Charles Henry tried to kill his wife in their back yard. She hadn't been drinking because her niece had been over all night, bringing that awful child with her that ran all over the place and pulled down everything he believed was a toy. He had tipped over the beautiful antique vase that she had brought home from a trip to Bali with her late husband. Her niece had just left with the boy when it happened.

When she heard the shot being fired.

Mrs. Berkeley had run to the window and looked across the street, then heard Nancy scream. She had also seen someone run across the yard. She hadn't seen his face since it was way too far away, but Nancy had told the police it was Charles.

So now she had stopped drinking. At least till the trial was over. The whole affair had become a media blast, and the last thing she wanted was for them to start digging into her life and finding all the empty bottles.

You can do this, Maria. You don't need a drink.

Mrs. Berkeley sighed and thought of George, her late husband. He hadn't liked her drinking either and always asked her to stop. She couldn't do it for him, and that tormented her now. If she couldn't do it for him, then how on earth was she supposed to do it for this?

You can do it!

She sipped her coffee and smacked her lips. Her white Miniature Schnauzer, Daisy, marched into the kitchen like she owned the entire place, and the world was there for her. She sat by Mrs. Berkeley's feet, her big brown eyes looking up at her.

"No, Daisy, not today. There are no more cookies. Vet says you're getting fat, remember?"

The dog wouldn't let it go. She knew that if she stared at her owner long enough, she would cave. And so it happened. Mrs. Berkeley sighed with a *tsk* after being stared at for a few minutes more, then walked to the cabinet and pulled out a box of cookies that her niece had baked and brought over when visiting a few days earlier.

"Here you go," she said and handed a cookie to the dog. She grabbed it, then took off with it in her mouth, tail wagging. Mrs. Berkeley chuckled. Why wouldn't she spoil the dog? She had so few years on this planet, and she should have the best.

And so should I.

Mrs. Berkeley lifted her nose toward the ceiling, suddenly feeling like she had been cheated out of something she had deserved. Why should these people be the judge of whether or not she was allowed to have a drink? It wasn't like one would hurt her.

"I only have a few more years left on this planet. I should be able to enjoy them," she mumbled and looked at her own reflection in the small mirror on the wall. She used her fingers to pull back her wrinkles, then licked her lips to make them look wet and less dried out.

No one will have to know.

Mrs. Berkeley strode back into the living room, but as soon as she walked through the door and her eyes met those of the very one she knew could only have come to kill her, she immediately regretted her desire to drink. Somehow, she had always suspected that her drinking would end up killing her one day; she had just never imagined it would happen like this.

Chapter 29

NANCY'S HANDS FELT CLAMMY, yet she was maintaining her perfect posture. She sat stiffly erect in the chair while the *Today* anchorman addressed the public through the camera. He was sitting across from her when he began to speak.

"My guest today is one I have to say I have the deepest admiration and respect for. What she had to endure is beyond anything I could ever imagine. Being kidnapped from your own house and being kept in a shed for five years, chained to a wall, eating and drinking out of bowls like a dog... If you are anything like me, dear viewer, then you are probably as appalled as I am by now and amazed that this woman survived."

The camera dollied back to include Nancy in the shot as well. The anchor's winter-blue eyes landed on her.

"Nancy Henry, you went through this ordeal. Tell us what happened, or rather what you remember because you suffered amnesia before or when you fell into the water that they pulled you out of."

"That is correct, Derek. I don't remember much. I suffered a blow to the back of my head and ended up somehow in the Sykes Creek River close to where I live. I don't know how I got there."

"But the police think someone tried to kill you and then threw you in that water, right?"

She nodded. "Yes. That is the theory."

"And who do they think did all this to you? Kidnapped you, keeping you in that shed…I think we have a picture here of the shed you were kept in and can bring it up on the big screen."

The picture of the shed appeared on the big flat-screen next to them, and a wave of shock went through the audience.

Derek clasped his mouth. "Dear Lord, Nancy. How on earth did you survive living in that place for…five years?"

Nancy looked down at her fingers, then up at the anchor. "I don't know, to be honest."

"And now the police have caught who did this to you, right?"

"That is correct."

"And tell us who he is."

Nancy lowered her eyes again and fiddled with her fingers. Then she cleared her throat to gather herself before she looked up.

"It was my husband."

"Your husband?" the anchor said, bursting it out, pretending not to have known this all along, like they didn't discuss it before she went on the show. Another wave of shock went through the audience, followed by a low murmur.

"So you mean to tell me, your own husband, the man you loved and whom you had two children with, kidnapped you and staged a home intrusion, then kept you in a shed for five years in a chamber of torture, I think we can all agree. I mean, look at it. It must have been burning hot during a Florida summer."

A frown made deep crease lines in his forehead and around his eyes. Nancy nodded while hiding behind a timid smile. A look of pain still flickered over her face. She straightened up and grabbed a tissue from the box placed in front of her. Derek pushed it closer, so she could better reach. She dabbed her eyes.

"And then he tried to kill you again, am I right?"

"Yes, I was found floating in Sykes Creek as you said, and some fishermen pulled me out."

"Barely alive, I imagine?"

He sounded shocked. The words crowded in her mouth and came out in a torrent.

"Yes. Those men saved my life. I had a lot of morphine inside me, and I would have drowned if they hadn't found me when they did."

"Real heroes," he said, his tone satisfied. "We still do have some left in this country; I am proud to say. Go on."

"Well, I came back and couldn't remember anything, and…"

"So, you couldn't even remember that it was your husband who had kept you in that shed, is that what you're saying?"

"Exactly. And so, I…well, I thought he still cared for me, and he let me stay in the guest cottage of our old house…"

She trailed off and lost her composure for a brief second before she managed to get herself back together again.

"He let you stay? But isn't that house yours too? You should be living in that house, especially with all you've been through?"

"Yes, but he had remarried and so…well…"

"He was playing the good guy, huh? Trying to make it look like he was at least fooling you once again, exploring the fact that you didn't remember that he was the one who had kept you in the shed for five years. Wow."

"Yes, and I am afraid I fell for it."

"And then he tried to kill you again? Tell us about that."

"Well, one day, I came back, actually on the night when the police had found the shed and taken me to see it."

"And you must have been out of it, right?"

"I was beginning to remember things when I saw the inside of the shed. I felt…I remembered it, yes."

"And so, he decided to try again?"

She nodded. "He…he came and fired a shot at me with his gun, then took off."

"So, he tried to kill you three times?"

She nodded. "Yes. That's what they believe."

"And that's what he is being charged with, right?"

Nancy cleared her throat again, then took a sip of water from the glass that some young guy with headphones on his neck had given her.

"Yes."

"And just what are you hoping to get out of it?"

She took in a deep breath. "Justice."

The anchorman leaned forward and placed a hand on her knee. "And if anyone deserves it, it is you. Good luck. We will all be rooting for you. Thank you for being here today."

The audience broke out in what seemed like spontaneous applause and stood to their feet, cheering her on, even long after the small camera lights had gone out.

"See, they're all with you, Nancy," Derek said as he took off the microphone. "The entire country is. We're all hoping that bastard will get what he deserves. I saw a hashtag trending on Twitter this morning called *#justiceforNancyHenry*. Your story is everywhere. There's no way a jury won't give him the death penalty. And rightfully so."

Nancy smiled, then shook his hand.

"Thank you."

She walked away, bouncing in her step. She, too, was beginning to believe that Charles would get exactly what he deserved.

Chapter 30

WE WATCHED Nancy's interview over breakfast. I was trying hard to listen in while my kids were screaming at one another, and Matt was doing his best to make them calm down. I was nervous for her as I feared she would break down on national television. She was so fragile.

I had advised her against doing the interview as I feared she was in no emotional state to follow through with it, but luckily, it went well. I turned off the TV in the kitchen and faced my family. It was Saturday and, for once, we actually had some time to spend together.

"So, will you get him convicted?" Olivia asked, half a pancake on its way into her mouth. Matt had made breakfast for all of us. He had spent the night, and Elijah had slept in Alex's room.

I glanced at Matt. We had been working, along with Roberts, on getting the case together these past two weeks since Nancy called me and told me Charles had tried to shoot her. We hadn't slept much nor had much time for each other or the children.

"I have a good feeling we will," I said. "We've done our part. Now, it's up to the court system. But I do feel pretty confident. The prosecutor says he believes it'll sail straight through."

"You're still nervous it won't?" Olivia asked.

I sipped my coffee and took a bite of my pancake. "Of course. There's always the doubt nagging inside you that it won't be enough or maybe that you got the wrong guy. It's part of the job."

"But you do have the right guy," Olivia said, wrinkling her forehead. "I mean, you heard what she said. He tried to kill her several times."

I nodded. "Yes, of course, we have the right guy. I was talking in general terms."

"Oh, okay."

"There's no doubt in me that he is guilty. We have so much on him," I continued. There was silence. I decided to fill it. "It really is a strong case against him."

Olivia nodded while eating.

I continued:

"First of all, the victim identified him. We have a witness, a neighbor seeing him flee the scene right after the shot was fired."

"Sounds good," Olivia said.

"And when it comes to that old story, the kidnapping of Nancy, we recently found out that Charles's alibi was Tanya, the woman who later became his wife. She told the police back then that she was with him all night at the office, working late. She stated that she was with him until he went home just before ten-thirty when he found the house empty and broken into. But a witness came forward and told us they had seen Tanya leave the office at eight o'clock that night. Her credit card was used at eight-thirty at a local gas station where a surveillance camera caught her getting out and walking into the shop. Also, and this hasn't been mentioned anywhere since we managed to keep it to ourselves for the trial, but another neighbor has come forward and told us he was out walking his dog. When he went past the Henrys' house at ten o'clock, he saw Charles' car parked in the driveway. He heard both Mr. and Mrs. Henry yelling at one another inside the house as he walked past it. He is completely certain it was Charles he heard. So, there you have it. We do have the right guy."

My daughter stared at me, eyes wide. "I didn't say you didn't."

"Gosh, Mom, you're so intense," Christine said. "Can't you ever just…chill out?"

With that, she grabbed her plate and walked out to the kitchen. I had been in a fight with her earlier in the morning, but I had to admit I didn't even remember what it was about. It was like everything had to be turned into a discussion these days, and everything I said could and would be used against me. I could barely open my mouth lately before someone told me what I said or did was wrong. It was becoming tiresome and a little exhausting.

"Can you believe her?" I asked Matt. He was engaged in something on his phone, scrolling away and tapping.

"Well, you were kind of intense back there," he finally said. "It was almost like you were trying to convince yourself."

"Excuse me? What is that supposed to mean?"

He shrugged, still without looking up from his phone. "Nothing. It's just that…I know it's bothering you."

"What is?"

Matt looked up finally. "That Charles is still claiming to be innocent."

He paused, and I sent him a brief glare of discontentment. He returned to his phone.

"Just forget it."

I looked after Christine as she disappeared up the stairs. I knew I wouldn't see her for the rest of the day unless she became hungry, and she'd walk down to grab something to eat, holding her computer in her hand, headphones on, watching those YouTube videos, barley noticing her surroundings. She never gave me anything but angry remarks. I felt like she was slipping away from me. I knew she was a teenager, but somehow, it seemed worse than it had been with Olivia when she was that age. The divorce and the death of her father probably didn't help.

And the fact that the baby was coming could only be making it worse. Was that why Christine was acting out? Was she nervous about it? Not knowing how life was going to be? Having a baby could be nerve-racking. Would I have enough time for her still? Would the house turn into a baby nightmare?

I was wondering about those things constantly, so it would only be natural if she were too.

I turned to look at Matt, who smiled while finishing his coffee. I felt my stomach and the baby, then once again wondered when we were going to have that discussion about our future. I had tried to bring it up a few times, but he kept avoiding the issue. Meanwhile, I thought about us a lot. Where would we live? Was there enough room in my house? Would we buy a new one? Could we afford it? And what about him and me? Were we going to marry? I wasn't an old-fashioned girl by any means, but when it came to having a child together, I believed you should be married. It just seemed better that way.

But Matt hadn't even mentioned it, and I didn't want to push it. Maybe he didn't want to get married?

We need to figure this out before the baby comes, at least. Doesn't he even think about it?

He lifted his eyes and met mine. I smiled, then sipped my coffee, deciding *not today*. We were having a nice peaceful morning for once, and I didn't want to ruin it.

Little did I know it would get ruined all by itself. As Matt smiled back, my phone buzzed on the table in front of me.

It was Roberts.

"I need you at Old Settlement Road. Now."

"At least say please."

He exhaled.

"Please?"

Chapter 31

"IT WAS the niece that found her. She came to visit as she often does on Saturdays, bringing her son. When Mrs. Berkeley didn't open the door, the niece walked right in, and that's where she found her."

Roberts walked up to the body and knelt next to her. Mrs. Berkeley was on her back, eyes staring into the ceiling. Techs were taking pictures and securing samples from her clothes.

"The knife was still in her abdomen when she was found," he continued. "Fifteen stabs."

"Someone was angry," I said and looked at the poor woman. I had come to know Mrs. Berkeley a little through the many interviews we had conducted, piecing together what she knew from the night Nancy disappeared, and helping her paint a picture of Nancy and Charles' relationship. She had been a tremendous help in building the case and was a key witness.

Losing her was going to be a big blow for us.

"If I were the type that cursed, then this would be the time I did it," I said and wiped the sweat from my forehead. I walked outside, feeling lightheaded and slightly nauseous. I wasn't as tough as I used to be, I had to admit. Or maybe it was just the pregnancy. Maybe I was just deeply frustrated.

I stood on Mrs. Berkeley's front porch, looking across the street at the Henrys' house. Roberts came up behind me.

"You think Charles killed her?"

I shrugged. "It would be the most obvious, but he's in police custody."

"He could have had help."

"Tanya?"

I paused after saying her name. She was going to be charged with perjury for lying to the police five years ago. But she was still free, out on bail before her trial. She was still living in the beautiful house across the street. She could easily have tried to help her husband out by removing the witness.

We had looked into Tanya's involvement in the whole affair, and I, for one, wanted her tried for accessory to attempted murder or attempted second-degree murder of Nancy Henry. Still, we didn't have enough to prove her involvement, unfortunately. I still didn't believe she couldn't have known. They had to have planned to get rid of Nancy together. If Charles had kept Nancy in that shed for five years and visited her to feed her and give her water, then chances were that Tanya knew about it too. But we had no evidence that would hold up in court, and the prosecutor had given up finding it. I, for one, believed it was still out there. I had tried to break her during interview after interview but never succeeded. I kept thinking that all I needed was a little more time, then she'd come around. I had a feeling she held a big part of the puzzle, and if we could only get it out of her, then we'd be home free. But not even when we promised her that she could walk free or at least receive a reduced sentence for her role in the kidnapping did she speak.

It tormented me.

"So, you want to pay her a visit?" Roberts said.

I started walking down the steps toward the road.

"Try and keep me away."

Chapter 32

THEN:

Jade started smoking. She was standing behind the house in the backyard down by the tall bushes, where no one could see her, blowing out smoke. She didn't really like the taste of it, nor did it make her feel good. Yet she did it anyway.

Jade pushed out smoke from between her lips, then blew a ring. A gust of light wind took it and destroyed it. Jade watched the smoke as it slid out over the water and disappeared. She felt her hands shaking, then smoked again.

"What do you think you're doing?"

Ethan!

Jade threw the cigarette in the water, then blew out the smoke, fast, waving it away. Her brother came through the bushes, hurrying toward her.

"Are you…smoking?"

She shook her head and hid the pack of cigarettes in her pocket.

"Yes, you were," he said. "Hand them over to me. Now."

She looked down, then pulled the cigarettes out of her pocket. His voice turned stiff as he spoke.

"Why would you do such a disgusting thing?"

She looked away, her eyes glaring out over the silver-gray water. A heron was walking in the shallow part, pecking for fish in the water.

"Jade? Answer me."

She didn't move.

He grabbed her shoulder. "Jade?"

She looked up at him, and their eyes met. His grew softer, and his shoulder eased.

"What's going on with you? I'm worried about you. You barely eat, you keep avoiding all of us, especially Mom, and you're constantly sulking. What's going on?"

She shook her head and pulled away from him. "Leave me alone."

"No, I won't, Jade. Something is off, and I can feel it. Dad is home, and you won't even talk to him. Don't you think that he senses something is wrong too? You're usually all over him when he gets back from one of his trips. You two are two peas in a pod. You have something special that I have always envied you."

"It's nothing, Ethan. Please. I promise."

But she didn't look at him when she said it. Him touching her shoulder made her shiver. She didn't like it when people touched her these days.

"Please. Just let me be alone, will you?"

"I don't think I can," he said, then reached out his hand. He held something inside of it. Jade's heart sank when she saw what it was.

"Care to explain?"

Tears sprang to her eyes. She wanted to run away, but where would she go? She was sixteen. She felt so adult, yet she was still so far making decisions about her own life. It didn't seem fair.

"Jade? Care to explain how I found a positive pregnancy test in the trash? I'm pretty sure it isn't Mom's."

Jade bit her lip, then turned away from him.

"I didn't even know you were having sex," he said. "I didn't even know you had a boyfriend? Tell me you told him?"

Jade's eyes landed on her toes in her flipflops. They needed new nail polish. Two of the toes had lost it completely, whereas others were only missing parts.

"Jade. You have to tell him."

She shook her head. A tear escaped her eye and landed on her big toe.

"Jade? Why won't you talk about this? Who is he? Tell me who he is."

Chapter 33

TANYA HENRY WASN'T HALF AS beautiful as the woman she had replaced. Where Nancy was tall, and her movements elegant like those of a gazelle, Tanya came off as a bad copy of her predecessor. It was almost like she was trying too hard to be like her. She kept her brown hair in a ponytail like Nancy, and she even wore a stylish blue dress like she usually would, but whereas Nancy's would seem elegant, Tanya's was short and showed too much cleavage. She was wearing so much make-up that it made her look like a doll.

"What do you want?" she asked as she opened the door. It was Saturday morning, yet she looked like she was going to a cocktail party in Miami. "I don't think we have anything more to say to one another."

"We need to ask you some questions," Roberts said.

"About what?"

I cleared my throat. "The death of Mrs. Berkeley across the street, Mrs.... do you still go by Henry?"

"Why wouldn't I?"

"Because, technically, you aren't married," I said. "Charles was already married to Nancy when he married you."

She lifted her nose toward the sky. "I am still Mrs. Henry. What happened to Mrs. Berkeley?"

"Can we come in?" Roberts asked.

"Why would you?"

"Or we could take you with us down to the station if you prefer," I said. "We could go in a patrol car so all the neighbors can see you. It's up to you."

She looked like one of my teenagers after I ask them to clean up their room. "All right then. Come on in."

We followed her inside the living room, where we sat down by a big table with room enough for around fifteen people. It was stunning and made from solid wood. Tanya didn't sit down; she stood by the window, looking into the big backyard overlooking the river where they had a boat docked. She took out a vape and started to smoke it. The air was soon filled with a sweet nauseating smell. I fought the urge to gag.

"So, what happened to the old hog across the street?" she asked and blew smoke out into the air. The room had high vaulted ceilings, yet the air around us soon became thick.

"The old...*hog* was murdered," I said.

Tanya was looking at her nails while I said it. I observed her reaction. It wasn't much, but I did see her flinch slightly. She remained composed, her manner businesslike, not allowing one sliver of emotion to escape.

"And just what exactly does that have to do with me?"

Roberts cleared his throat. "Well, since you are one who would benefit from her passing, we thought it appropriate to..."

She smoked and stared at Roberts, narrowing her eyes. "So, you think I did it. To get my husband out of jail, is that it?"

"That is it," I said.

"Sounds like a cheap mystery novel to me," she said, still studying her newly manicured nails, turning them in the sunlight from the window.

"Maybe, but you must admit you have a motive," I said. "Where were you last night?"

She pulled her lips into a smile. "I was here, crying over the loss of the man I love. Devastated over the fact that he is probably going to jail for something he didn't do, and our life together is ruined. Does that count as an alibi?"

I shrugged. "If you did it with someone."

She lifted her gaze and met my eyes across the room.

"I didn't. I was alone. Just like I will be from now on if you don't give up this crazy idea that my husband could harm anyone, let alone his ex-wife."

"What do you make of her?" Roberts asked me as we had left the house and walked down the driveway. "I, for one, think she's lying through her teeth. I believe she's been lying to us ever since the beginning."

I turned to look at him, feeling grief for the loss of Mrs. Berkeley as her body was taken out of the house on a stretcher. A small group of neighbors had gathered in the street.

"I don't know," I said. "All I know is that being in there gave me a tremendous headache."

"It was probably the smoke. I can't stand vapes. The smell is worse than smoke from a cigarette, and to be honest, I prefer the old-fashioned types. It makes me so angry that she would smoke in the presence of a pregnant woman."

I forced a smile and nodded. "Yeah, that's probably it."

Chapter 34

"COULD you stop looking at your phone?"

That same night, Matt took me out for dinner at Djon's, a high-end place in Melbourne Beach, and one of our favorites. It was a nice evening, the lights dim, and the food super delicious. Still, I couldn't get Mrs. Berkeley out of my mind and kept glancing at my phone to see if Roberts might have tried to get in contact with me. I had told him to let me know if the techs found anything that could lead us to her murderer. I was angry and had almost canceled dinner, but Matt had planned this weeks ago, so it wouldn't be fair to him.

"I'm sorry," I said and pushed it away. The piano player played a song by Elton John so smoothly it almost became annoying. Maybe it just didn't fit my state of mind. "I can't help myself. Someone murdered that poor Mrs. Berkeley, and I can't let it go."

He reached out his hand and touched mine. "Try anyway. For me."

I smiled and looked deep into his eyes. "Oh, baby. I am ruining this entire evening for you. I am so sorry. We're finally alone, and now I'm just preoccupied." I turned the phone over, so the screen faced the tablecloth, then looked at him again, holding his hand. "I'm all yours, baby."

We clinked glasses, mine with soda in it, then drank. The waiter arrived with our appetizers. I was having the seafood crepe while Matt had the King Crab spring rolls. All of it was excellent and literally melted on the tongue. But I worried it was too expensive.

"So…Matt," I said, thinking this would be a good time to start addressing our future plans. It had to be done.

"Yes?" he said with a blissful smile.

I bit my lip, not certain I wanted to ruin the moment. He seemed so happy right now. I didn't want to destroy that.

But if you don't say anything now, you never will.

"Nothing…it was just nothing."

"Sure, it was something, Eva Rae," he said. "Go on."

"I was just thinking that…we should talk about, well, the…" I touched my stomach, thinking he might understand what I meant.

"Okay," he said. "I was thinking Hector if it's a boy. I had a friend in elementary school by that name, and I always liked it."

Hector? Where did that come from all of a sudden?

"Are you serious? As in the boy who put his own fist so far down his throat during math class that he threw up?"

Matt nodded. "Yeah, you do remember him. I didn't think you did."

"You're kidding me, right?"

He put his fork down, and his expression became hurt.

"Oh, dear, you're not kidding?"

"I like Hector. Don't you?"

Be honest, Eva Rae, or you'll lead him on, and he won't let it go. Be honest!

"No, it's great…really."

I sipped my Fanta, thinking we had a long way to go. I had thought we were going to talk about moving in together, how to solve our living arrangements, and possibly—hopefully—a marriage.

That's what I wanted to talk about.

He just wanted to name our kid Hector?

Suddenly, I wondered if we were too far apart. Didn't he know how badly I wanted to be married? Was that why hadn't he proposed?

Didn't he know me at all?

Chapter 35

"YOU'RE ANGRY."

I shook my head. "No, honey. I just have a lot on my mind; that's all."

"Come on, Eva Rae. We've known each other since pre-school. I know when you're angry. You have that look."

If you know me so well, how do you not know what I really want?

Everything was suddenly screaming inside of me, and I wanted most of all just to leave.

He leaned back in the chair, his fingers tapping lightly on the white tablecloth. "You're angry at me because I like the name Hector, am I right?"

I felt how my eyes grew wider, and I chewed aggressively. Was he for real right now? It had nothing to do with that stupid name. Could he really not see that?

"You don't like the name Hector, is that why?"

I rubbed my forehead, closing my eyes. "No, Matt. That's not why."

He stared at me. I felt awful. It was suddenly like the food was growing inside my mouth, making it hard to swallow.

"Maybe we should talk when we get home," I said.

He reached out his hands in the air and raised his voice slightly, just enough for it to be embarrassing in the nice quiet atmosphere.

"No, Eva Rae. Why can't you just tell me now? If what I have said or done is so terrible, why not just tell me right away?"

I swallowed a bite of my crepe. "All right. If you really want to know, I'm angry because I'm pregnant and you haven't proposed to me. There, you have it."

I fought my urge to burst into tears. With the hormones raging inside of me and the anger over the day's events, and Matt's avoidance of the real issue, I knew it wouldn't last long. There was just a little too much right now for one pregnant woman to handle.

Matt sat back in his chair, mouth gaping.

"Can you blame a girl for wanting to get married?" I asked, dropping my fork on the plate. "For wanting you to make an honorable woman of her? Call me old fashioned, but certain things should be the way they used to be."

Now, the tears were welling up in my eyes, and I wiped them away with my napkin, dabbing my eyes, trying not to smear the make-up, trying to keep the little of my pride that I had left.

He stared at me, hands folded in front of him. He was shaking his head slowly, smacking his lips.

"Say something, Matt. You're making me nervous here. What's going on?"

He shook his head again, then grumbled something I couldn't hear.

"Matt?"

"You sure are something, Eva Rae. You sure are something."

"What do you mean? I'm not following you here?"

He leaned forward, clenching his fist on the table. "You gotta be the most annoying woman ever to have set foot on this earth."

"That wasn't exactly the reaction I was going for from you," I said.

"By far the most irritating..."

"What's going on here? Why are you acting like this?"

The clenched fist was pushed closer to me, then opened with the palm turned up. Inside lay the most beautiful ring with a gorgeous diamond on top.

My heart dropped. My throat closed up, and I could barely breathe.

"Oh, dear Lord, Matt. You were going to propose? Tonight?"

He nodded, his jaws clenched.

"And you had it all planned out. That's why you wanted to take me to dinner here, in our favorite place, and then you…you were just waiting for the right moment?"

He nodded again while rolling his tongue against the inside of his cheek.

"And now I've ruined it?"

Chapter 36

A LONG SILENCE grew between us. The waiters brought the entrees, but we had both lost our appetites. Finally, I mustered the courage to speak.

"I am so sorry, Matt. You must believe me. I never meant to..."

He threw out his arms. "You never do, do you? Mean to ruin everything, yet you do it...all the time."

"Excuse me?"

He sniffled and sipped his wine. His eyes were avoiding mine. He was fuming, and it felt like he just couldn't look at me. That's how angry he was.

"How was I supposed to know?" I asked, trying to keep my voice low, so the entire restaurant didn't hear us. "That you were going to propose tonight?"

"I have planned this for a very long time," Matt said, doing his best to keep it low too, but not succeeding.

"I didn't know that. I thought you didn't care. I thought you didn't even want to get married. Why didn't you do it sooner? It's been months? I am five months pregnant, almost six. Don't tell me you didn't have time."

"But when did you want me to do it? When you granted me five minutes of your precious time in between your cases? Or when you came home from the shelter? You're never home, Eva Rae. We're never together because you don't prioritize us."

"I have been busy with this case over the past few weeks, yes, but before that, there was plenty of time. Don't give me that. Don't make this my fault."

"But it is your fault. It takes time to plan something like this. Just finding the right ring took forever, then I had to save the money for it. And not to mention the weeks I spent finding the courage."

"Oh, dear God, I am a fool," I said. "I should just have kept my stupid mouth shut. How about I just pretend like I don't know anything, and we start all over?"

"Don't patronize me. I am not one of your children," Matt said. He was getting tipsy now. I could hear it in his slurred speech. He never did tolerate wine very well. He was a beer man, and the strong alcohol in wine always got to him. "It's not some board game where we can just start all over again from scratch."

"I realize that, but…does it matter? I mean, you have the ring. We both want this…and it is an awfully beautiful ring…"

I reached across the table to grab his hand in mine.

He pulled his out of my grip. "Of course, it matters."

I pulled back. "But…why?"

"Because you always do this. You always control everything and make me seem like a lesser person. This was my thing. I was in control of this, yet you somehow managed to make me look like a fool. You're always telling me what to do, when to do it, controlling everything and everyone. Meanwhile, you can't even control your own eating habits. Slobbering over hot dogs, gobbling them down with sodas. Meanwhile, you're getting bigger and bigger, and I can't stand it. You think I need to be controlled? How about you control yourself?"

I sank back in my seat. I stared at Matt, unable to find words. Was that how he felt about me?

Matt stared at me, and I could tell he immediately regretted his words. He had said too much, but it was too late now.

"Eva Rae…I…"

"Wow. That was a lot. It sounds like you've been carrying this for quite some time. Gathering up faults. I bet it felt good finally to get it off your chest."

"No…Eva Rae…it didn't…"

"Don't. Don't even try."

I grabbed my phone and put it in my purse, then got up, biting back my tears.

"See you around, Matt."

Chapter 37

THE LAWYER'S voice echoed off the wooden walls in his office. Nancy stared at him, unable to fathom what had left his lips. Had she heard him right? Could it really be? Or was she imagining things?

"Nancy? Did you hear what I said?"

Nancy blinked. She looked down at her fingers, then back up at him behind the big mahogany desk. His glasses had slid down his nose, and he glared at her from above the rims.

"I...I..."

Mike Jenkins smiled. It wasn't quite as bright and spectacular as the one on his poster by I95 that Nancy had passed on her way to his office, but still enough to dazzle any jury in a court of law, as he was known to do. He was the best divorce lawyer around, and she knew of several women who had gotten extremely favorable settlements by using him.

"That's all you have to say? I just told you that you got everything you wanted, and this is what I get?"

"Yes...I mean no, I'm sorry...I'm just a little..."

"Surprised? Well, so am I," he said, "But I have it here in black and white. He's giving up the house and half of everything he owns."

"Just like that?" Nancy asked.

"Well, I had to fight for it at first, but I think Charles just didn't want it to go to court. That's why he decided to settle. So there you have it, in a matter of a few weeks, you'll be legally divorced."

"And you're telling me that...the house..."

"It's yours. To be fair, half of it has always been yours. But now you won't have to sell it unless you want to, of course."

Nancy lifted her gaze.

"And Tanya?"

"Their marriage is illegal in the eyes of the law," he said. "There's no way any judge will see it otherwise, and it will be annulled. With your divorce, the two of them are free to marry again if they want to. But my guess is she won't want to once he gets sentenced to death row. She risks a prison sentence, too, for the perjury case. She might not have known what he was up to, but she helped him by lying and giving him an alibi. It doesn't look good for her, either. Right now, the police are trying to determine just how involved she was."

Nancy sipped the cup of coffee that Mike's secretary had served her. It was still early in the morning, and she wasn't a morning person, never had been. She always felt a little lightheaded the first few hours, but now she was suddenly feeling very clear in her mind.

"Finally, a little good news, huh?" he said. "I have to say it has been my pleasure to help you get the most out of this ordeal. After what he did to you...I just can't imagine what could make a husband act that way. He will get what he deserves, and we will all be clapping when he is sentenced; trust in that."

Nancy smiled secretively. She was hearing this a lot from people these days. There was so much support. Letters arrived every day at her small condo she had rented in north Merritt Island, the cheapest she could find since she had no money, and the little she had went to her lawyer. People were constantly pouring their sympathies on her, especially after her appearance on the *Today Show*. And the phone was ringing with modeling jobs, as she was now the hottest woman in Florida, not to mention the Hollywood producers who were right now fighting over the rights to her story, throwing big numbers at her other lawyer. She was never going to be poor again; that was the goal. With the settlement came a sum of two million dollars, half of everything Charles owned, and the house. She couldn't forget that. She had dreamt of living there again with the stunning river views.

Things were beginning to shape up for her.

Finally.

Chapter 38

THE TV WAS ON, but I wasn't paying attention. Instead, I was sitting with my phone in hand, staring at the screen like I could somehow mentally will Matt to call and say he was sorry. Still, the phone remained quiet as the grave, and I was eating Oreos straight out of the box.

It had been two days since Matt and I quarreled, and I hadn't left the couch except to feed the children and make sure they got to school.

Around noon, Melissa rang my doorbell. I hadn't seen her in a long while, but as soon as I did, I struggled to keep myself composed.

"Oh, dear, sweetheart," she said as I threw myself in her arms, getting one of her famous warm hugs. "I got your text. What a mess, huh?"

She grabbed my hand in hers, and we walked to the living room where she saw the half-eaten box of Oreos on the couch and the crumbs circling the area where I had been sitting.

"Oh, it's bad; I see," she said. "Let me make us some coffee."

"Is it too early for red wine?" I said with a sniffle.

She tilted her head and looked at my stomach. "A little bit. And maybe not the best to be drinking alcohol right now."

"I knew I should have called my sister instead," I grumbled and threw myself on the couch while Melissa disappeared into the kitchen to make the coffee. But I didn't mean it. I had called Melissa because she was the one who always took care of all of us, and especially of me. When growing up, we had been a tight-knit group of four people: me, Matt, Melissa, and Dawn. Melissa was the mom of the group, the one who always made sure we had a ride home when we went places and that we didn't forget to plan for where to eat dinner.

"Here you go," she said and placed a warm mug in my hands. I felt a wave of gratefulness wash over me. Of course, this was exactly what I needed right now. And, of course, Melissa knew this.

"You're a lifesaver," I said and sipped it. "I couldn't even find the energy to make myself a cup of coffee. How pathetic is that?"

"You're pregnant and just broken up with your boyfriend. Looking at the box of Oreos, I think we're beyond pathetic."

I sent her a smile, and she plopped down next to me on the couch, grabbed an Oreo, and put it in her mouth. "So, tell me everything. What kind of a pig has Matt been this time?"

Thinking about that night again made my eyes well up. "He wanted to propose to me, and…"

I paused when I saw something on the screen that suddenly caught my interest.

"He wanted to propose?" Melissa said. "Oh, the bastard."

I stared at the screen, and Melissa saw me doing it, then turned her interest to the TV as well.

"Say, isn't that woman…what's her name…?"

"Nancy. Nancy Henry," I said.

"Yes, you were on her case, weren't you? Do you know her? Now, what that husband did to her, that makes me…"

"I want to hear this," I said and reached for the remote. I turned the volume up high and listened.

"She got the house?" Melissa said after we had listened to the reporter for a few seconds. "Good for her."

"And two million dollars," I said.

"I say she deserves every penny, and even more. If anyone kept me locked up in a shed for five years, I'd demand a lot more. Just sayin'."

Melissa paused and looked at me for a response.

"Why do you look like that?" she said.

"Like what?"

"Like you're not thrilled for her?"

"I don't look like that."

"Yes, you do. I know that look in your eyes."

"I don't have any look in my eyes," I said and sipped more coffee. "I'm just listening carefully."

Melissa shook her head. "Could have fooled me."

She grabbed another Oreo and bit into it.

"You almost had me thinking you were having doubts about her, and whether or not Charles Henry is innocent. But I guess that's just me. Right?"

Chapter 39

THEN:

"You mean to tell me that he took you into a room and gave you a massage while you were naked under the towel?"

Jade sniffled and wiped her eyes. They had walked up to the house and were sitting outside in the patio furniture. Ethan was panting and agitated, and his skin was getting flushed. His nostrils were flaring, making her feel uncomfortable. She didn't like to upset him.

"I'm to blame too, Ethan. Please, don't be mad."

"You're to blame? You're to blame?" he shook his head. "Where does this even come from?"

She breathed raggedly and looked at her feet. "I led him on. I didn't tell him not to massage me."

Ethan rose to his feet with a loud groan. "You led him on? Can't you hear how insane that sounds? Has he told you this? Is he telling you that you're guilty in this? Is he telling you that you wanted this, that you somehow made him do this to you?"

She shook her head. "No, Ethan, it wasn't like that."

"You're sixteen, for crying out loud. He's an adult. He holds the responsibility. He shouldn't even have suggested it."

"Please, don't be mad," she said, now crying hard.

Seeing this, Ethan eased up. He knelt in front of her, grabbing her hands between his. She was shaking.

"No, no, oh, sweet sis. Don't for one minute think that I am mad at you. You're not to blame here. Do you hear me? Look at me, Jade."

He placed a finger under her chin and lifted her head so she could look him in the eyes. Then he smiled comfortingly.

"We'll figure this out together, do you hear me? I will not let him do this to you and get away with it."

She nodded, then swallowed. She had this big lump growing in her throat that kept getting bigger the more he reassured her that everything would be okay. He sat next to her on the patio swing.

"I'll take care of you, sis; you can trust in that."

"I do, Ethan, but what are we going to do? I can't have a baby. I won't do it. I'm too young."

He nodded. "We'll deal with that. But first, we have to do one thing."

"What's that?"

"We need to tell Mom. She needs to know."

Jade pulled her hands out of his grip and turned away. "No, Ethan. I…I can't."

"But, you have to."

"How do you expect me to look into her eyes and tell her this? You know how fond she is of Billy?"

"Even the more reason for her to know. She needs to confront him about it, and then she'll take care of you. But Billy needs to go. He needs to get out of our lives, and the only way you can make her do that is to tell."

Jade shook her head violently, then rose to her feet. "I can't, Ethan. I won't do it."

"You must, Jade. There's no way around it."

Crying, Jade turned around and took off running. As she reached the end of the yard, she heard her brother yell behind her:

"If you don't, then I will. Do you hear me, Jade? JADE?"

Chapter 40

NANCY SAW her as she drove up the driveway in her new Cadillac Escalade that she had bought only the day before after receiving the money from Charles. Tanya was standing on the front porch, vaping. She had two suitcases standing next to her. She had her things, the few that were hers from the house, taken away by the movers the night before. Nancy wondered for a second if she had found somewhere to live. It was short notice.

Nancy took a deep breath, gathering herself as she opened the SUV door and got out. She didn't have much, only a small box with things and a suitcase with clothes. It was strange to own practically nothing since Charles had thrown out most of her stuff, except for some clothes he had put in the attic.

Nancy grabbed the box in her arms and walked to the end of the stairs. Tanya looked down at her, blowing out smoke.

"I guess you're feeling pretty good about yourself, huh?" she said. "Nothing in there is how you left it. Everything is new. Charles bought new couches, a new bed, even new plates. I told Charles I wasn't going to live in your belongings, and he agreed. We needed to get rid of every sign of you. It might look like your house from the outside, but it's not. It stopped being yours years ago."

Nancy swallowed. The agreement said the house with its belongings. She had wanted it that way because she wanted it to be exactly like it used to be. She hadn't thought about the fact that they might have changed it completely.

The look in Tanya's eyes was deadly. She truly hated her and wasn't even trying to hide it.

"Tanya…"

She shook her head. "Don't talk to me. I'm just staying here until my cab comes. Apparently, the cars were both in Charles' name, and since I am not married to him anymore, then…"

"He fooled us both, Tanya," Nancy said, taking a couple of steps up toward her. Tanya shook her head, smoking, avoiding looking at Nancy as she reached the landing.

"You tell yourself what you want to, but I will never believe you. I don't believe for one second that Charles would have kidnapped you and held you captive in that shed. No matter what you say."

"But, Tanya, don't you see? He fooled the entire world—you, the kids, everyone. He made them believe I was kidnapped or had been killed in a home invasion. I didn't want to believe it either, but then he tried to kill me. You heard the shot that night. He stood over there by the guesthouse and pointed the gun at me, then fired it. I was just lucky he missed."

Tanya glared at her, then shook her head. "I still don't believe it. You're lying or remembering it wrong. Charles would never do that."

"That's what I used to say too. I used to love him like you obviously do. I was smitten by his charm and the look in his eyes. The way he smiled when looking at me was the best part. It lit up his entire face. There was nothing better than seeing him light up like that when I entered the room. I thought he loved me. I believed in him and me. But he's a sociopath, Tanya. He almost got away with kidnapping me and later trying to kill me. Meanwhile, he played the devoted husband to you and father to my children, saddened by the loss of his wife. It's sick, Tanya. He is a very sick man."

There was a glint of something in Tanya's eyes that made Nancy believe she was reaching her, or at least a small part of her, but a moment later, it was gone. A car drove up behind her.

Tanya put the vape away, then lifted up her suitcases. "One of these days, Nancy, the world will realize what a liar you are, and you'll get what you deserve. Just you wait and see. Enjoy the house; please try not to break anything. I want it perfect for when I come back."

Chapter 41

MELISSA LEFT, and I cuddled up under the blanket, glaring at my phone on the table. Did I even want Matt to call me? I was so furious at him for the things he said; I wasn't sure I would be able to speak to him. He knew my weight was my weakness. He knew how much it would hurt me to say those things. Was that the point of it? Or was he simply just not happy with me being this way? Because having a child doesn't usually make you skinnier afterward, and I hoped he realized that.

Was Matt really that superficial?

I got up, walked to the kitchen to get myself a glass of water, then returned to the couch, and sat down. I looked at my phone's display again to see if he had texted me while I was gone, but nothing.

Should I text him?

I was, after all, the one who left him in the restaurant. Maybe I should be the one to reach out first? Was that what he was waiting for?

Or had he just given up?

I felt so confused, and I wanted so terribly to go back to that dinner and take everything back that I had said. If only I hadn't spoken about proposing. If only I hadn't emasculated him like that. He needed to be in control of this. He needed to feel like a man. It was only natural.

"Since when did things become so complicated?"

I groaned the words out in my living room. I rubbed my forehead and closed my eyes while thinking about the baby. Would Matt and I be able to mend the pieces? It would be easier to quit now than to start over again. We could share custody. But was it the life I wanted for my unborn? At least my three others had their dad living with them while growing up.

For crying out loud, Matt. Stop being proud. Call and tell me you're sorry, and you didn't mean it.

I sniffled and sipped my glass when the phone on my table buzzed. Startled at this, I spilled a few drops of water on my PJs before putting it down. I wiped them off with one hand, then reached for the phone with the other, my heart pounding in my chest.

The display said, Roberts.

Dang it!

I closed my eyes in disappointment and pinched the bridge of my nose, pushing it back, ...all the anger and resentment. Why couldn't it have been him?

"Yes?"

"Thomas," Roberts said. "I don't quite know how to tell you this."

"Really? Not many people say that these days, they usually just blurt out the truth without considering my feelings."

"Eh...?"

"Sorry. That was personal. What's going on?"

"I have emailed you a report. It's from the forensic's office. Take a look at it. I have to say it doesn't look good."

"What? What do you mean?"

"Just read it, and then we'll talk, okay?"

Chapter 42

NANCY ENJOYED BEING HOME. It wasn't true what Tanya had said, that it was no longer her house. The furniture and the things in the cabinets and drawers might be new, but the old house still felt very much like hers.

"Finally," she groaned as she sat down in a rocking chair by the window overlooking the river, where the sun was beginning to set. The sky was painted in a gorgeous pink, and Nancy was taken back to her life before the incident. She and Charles used to sit and watch the sunsets together. Well, before the kids came, of course. After that, everything changed. They got busy, and there was no sitting still. It was only natural; that's the way it went, yet she couldn't help missing those days when things were simple. Back when they could wait till late before deciding what they'd have for dinner—if they'd go out or cook together in their big kitchen. It had been brand new back then, and it was Nancy's favorite part of the house. Charles and Tanya had remodeled it, and as Nancy walked out there to look, she barely recognized it. It was all white now and modern. No more granite countertops at the breakfast bar where the kids sat and ate, spilling milk and cereal. Everything was now black and white, with surfaces so clean, Nancy wondered if Tanya had ever cooked a meal in there.

Nancy touched the counter and ran a finger across it. She walked back to the living room and stood in front of the end wall, then touched it gently, letting a flat palm caress it in the place where the blood had been. It had been cleaned and painted over, probably more than once since they renovated the kitchen.

Nancy gasped lightly, then turned away from it. She was breathing raggedly now as some of the memories came back to her. She grabbed hold of the back of the couch and leaned on it while the images rushed through her: the fist punching her face, her falling back into the wall behind. Her fighting to stay conscious as he grabbed her shirt and pulled her up, screaming in her face, then punching her again and again. As she closed her eyes, she could still feel the pain from it.

Fighting to breathe, Nancy let go of the couch and decided to go outside. Too many thoughts and memories were crowding her mind now, and she couldn't stand it. It was too much. Too heavy.

Nancy walked out on the porch. She suddenly didn't care for the quietness of the house. She had wanted to call her children and ask them to come down for the weekend, but she didn't dare to. They were so busy. And probably still angry with her. She knew they thought she was framing their dad. They didn't believe her story.

Hopefully, they'll come around.

Nancy found a patio chair and sat down with a deep sigh. The air felt fresh. A cold spell was going to cover the state tomorrow, and the wind had already started to blow from the north. She loved those temperature drops that came like a friend in the night and left the air fresh and crisp for a couple of days.

Nancy took a deep breath and filled her lungs with the clean air.

It felt so good finally to be home.

As she smiled at the thought, her phone buzzed in her pocket. She pulled it out and looked at the display, then almost dropped it again. She stared at the words on the screen, heart pounding in her chest.

YOU SHOULDN'T HAVE DONE THAT

Chapter 43

I WAS RUSHING DOWN the street, stepping on the accelerator, and making it through the intersection on a yellow light. Alex's toy truck on the passenger seat fell to the floor with a thud and landed in the old Five Guys' bag from three days ago. I really ought to clean up my car one of these days, I thought to myself.

But not today.

What Roberts had shown me kept rolling over in my mind. I couldn't believe my own eyes as I saw the report. I wasn't sure what to think anymore.

Matt's car was in the driveway as I drove up and parked. It was late now, but not so late that he would tell me to wait until tomorrow. I couldn't wait. I had to tell him about the report. I had to push through this awful feeling inside of me and talk to him. As I got out, I wondered if I should have texted him that I was on my way. I hadn't done that since I didn't want him to tell me to stay away. I didn't want him to tell me I could just tell him via text, that there was no need to talk face to face.

I wanted to see him. I wanted to look into his eyes and see if he really hated me so much, like it had seemed when he said those awful things, or if there was still some love left in them.

Maybe we can mend the broken pieces? Maybe we can somehow find our way back? Please, Matt, please, be gentle with my heart.

I took a deep breath to calm down the jitters in my stomach, then knocked on the door.

There was a noise from the other side, and I prepared myself to look into his eyes again, hoping that it wouldn't feel weird or uncomfortable. The door swung open, and I opened my mouth to speak.

"Matt…I…"

Then I stopped. It wasn't Matt who had opened it. It was someone else.

A woman.

She smiled. She was wearing a tank top showing a lot of skin.

"Yes? Who are you?" she chirped.

A surprised voice came up behind her, and I saw Matt's face. His hair was a mess, his eyes branded with shame.

"E-Eva Rae?"

Realizing that Matt knew me, the woman walked back inside and let Matt come to the door. He paused. I could hear his breathing. It was quick and shallow.

"W-what are you doing here?"

There was a different quality to his voice now. It became haunted, saturated with guilt.

"I didn't know you were coming over?"

I blinked, pressing back tears. "I see that."

My voice was cracking, so I stopped talking. I didn't want him to hear how upset I was, how deeply he had hurt me.

"Oh, no, Eva Rae, you…why didn't you call before you came over?"

"Oh, I see. How unthoughtful of me," I said, taking a step back, away from him. I couldn't deal with this right now, with him or us, if there were an "us" left. "I am so sorry that I didn't call or text you first."

"Argh, you're so…you're so…" he said. His voice was cold, almost angry now. Tears were stinging in the back of my eyes. I wouldn't be able to hold them back much longer.

"Lorraine is…"

I lifted my eyebrows. "Lorraine, huh?"

"Eva Rae, listen…I…we were having a fight and…you were angry with me. I thought we were over…"

So, that's why he hasn't called.

I shook my head. "And you just moved on, huh? She's definitely pretty. And it doesn't look like she eats much junk food either. She doesn't have any fat on that body; that's for sure. And we all know how much you dislike that, huh?"

"Eva Rae, don't be mad, please?"

My stomach was a hard ball by now. The knot in my throat was threatening to explode. I couldn't let him see it. I had suffered big enough of a defeat tonight. He wasn't having this as well.

"I should…I should probably…go."

"Why do you always have to be like this?" Matt yelled after me.

I turned around and hurried to the car. Matt called my name, but I didn't stop. I backed out of the driveway, swung the car into the street, then took off, biting back tears along with what was left of my pride.

Chapter 44

THE BOTTLE WAS ALREADY ALMOST empty, and Nancy didn't understand how that could have happened. She had opened the white wine just a short while ago. Could she have emptied it already?

She lifted it and put it up in the light coming from inside her living room. She was sitting out on the porch overlooking the Indian River. The No-See-Ums were biting, but she barely noticed anymore.

She poured the last drops into her glass then drank them before placing the glass on the small round patio table. She was drunk now, no doubt about it. Her head was spinning and buzzing, competing with the cicadas sitting in the trees around her. Charles had let them grow too big, she thought. They blocked the view—especially the old magnolia at the end of the yard. It needed trimming.

Nancy would see to it.

She stared at her phone and the text she had received earlier. They didn't scare her with their little texts. She wasn't afraid, not after what she had been through. But the words did hurt her.

Nancy sighed, then leaned back in the rocking chair, closing her eyes, breathing in the moist air. Being back didn't fill her with as much joy as she had expected. The house was different somehow now. It felt different.

Perhaps Tanya is right? The house no longer belongs to me?

Maybe she should sell it. Make a good sum, and then just take off. Get out of this awful place? Buy a cute house in the Smokey Mountains?

Nancy shook her head. She had finally succeeded in getting her house back. It seemed silly to give up just like that.

Give it time, Nancy. Give it time.

She opened her eyes and looked at the empty bottle. Her head was going to hurt tomorrow, yet she still wanted more. She rose to her feet and walked to the kitchen. She had put several bottles in the fridge and pulled out another one. She popped it open, then poured herself another glass. She gulped it down almost in one sip, then poured herself some more. She closed the fridge, then staggered with the bottle in her hand, the glass in the other, through the kitchen.

As she kicked the door open and walked through to the living room, she saw the shadowy figure standing by the back door. She squinted her eyes to make sure he was really there. He was wearing a hoodie, so she couldn't see his face.

"What do you want?" she asked. Her voice was slurred. She could hear it herself. That's how bad it was.

The gun in his hand startled her, and she dropped the bottle. It fell to the tiles but didn't shatter. Wine gushed out on her feet.

"Please," she said.

"I told you not to do what you did," the voice said. "I warned you. I don't want to hurt you, but you leave me no choice."

The voice sounded ragged and in distress. Nancy stared at the gun, then shook her head and walked backward.

"Why did you come back?" the voice said. "Why?"

"This is my house," Nancy said. "You have no right to come here and…and…"

The shadow stepped closer, the gun shaking in their hand. It was cocked, and Nancy could barely breathe. She looked toward the door, then wondered if she would be able to make it if she sprang for it.

She didn't think about it twice. She started to run, dropping the glass in her other hand, and just took off, sprinting.

Chapter 45

I WAS SPEEDING while listening to Panic at the Disco, turning the volume up high. I was singing but might also have been screaming while driving over the bridge toward Merritt Island.

"Lorraine? Matt? Lorraine? Really?"

I was crushed. I hadn't realized that we were this bad off. I thought we had a fight. A serious one, yes, one that had ended up hurting us both. But we weren't in a place where we couldn't mend the broken pieces. Not in my opinion. But, apparently, to Matt, we were all over? We were so far out we couldn't fix it?

And just like that, he had moved on? How did anyone do that this fast?

I stopped at a red light when reaching the island, then touched my stomach gently. How were we going to manage to be parents with everything that was going on? My ex-husband had cheated on me and left me for another woman. Was that what Matt had done here? Cheated on me? Did it count as cheating? In my book, it did. We had a fight. We hadn't ended things or been on a break like Ross and Rachel in *Friends*. This was clear in my mind, but apparently not in his?

Why are you making excuses for him?

If there was one thing I had no tolerance for, it was men who cheated on me. That was the end of it. Matt and I were through as of this evening; we were no longer a couple. Then we'd have to figure out how to deal with the baby and how to share custody. I didn't want my child to grow up without a father. I had three who were doing just that after their dad died, and it broke my heart to see how much they missed him—especially Alex, who was so young, and who needed a male role model in his life.

I drove up South Tropical Trail. The road in front of me was dark, and the Spanish Moss hanging from the trees covering the road looked like fingers reaching for me. I cried but kept pushing it back. I didn't want to cry over him. I didn't want to think about how it could have been. Nagging guilt kept creeping into my mind, telling me it was my fault, that I pushed him away. If only I had let him propose in his own timing. If only I hadn't jumped the gun the way I did and ruined everything.

I drove past the small white Georgianna church that marked the beginning of Old Settlement Road. It had fresh flowers on the porch. I drove past Mrs. Berkeley's house and stopped across the street from it, by the Henrys' house that now belonged to Nancy. I stared at Mrs. Berkeley's empty windows and the crime scene tape, then felt such deep sadness. The poor woman. Then I wondered for a second about the shot she had heard the night that Nancy disappeared. I still couldn't figure out where that bullet had gone. Who fired a gun and then cleaned up after themself? Was it Charles? It had to have been, right?

Then I thought about the information Roberts had given me earlier in the day. Something was way off in this story, and I couldn't really get to the bottom of it. I hoped Nancy could help me do just that. I had also hoped that Matt would be by my side when I confronted her with it, but that's not how it was going to be.

While I was pondering this, walking up to the front door, I heard a noise come from inside Nancy's house. It sounded like glass breaking, and then it was followed by a scream.

Chapter 46

NANCY SCREAMED. The intruder was faster than her and ran to grab her. She felt his arm around her neck and was pulled back forcefully before she reached the door. Nancy screamed as she was dragged across the floor.

"Please, please," she said, fear tearing through her voice.

"I warned you," the intruder yelled, then threw her on the floor. She hurt her head as it slammed against the wooden floors. "I warned you not to come back!"

"But...please..."

He stood above her, pointing his finger at her face. "No. You don't get to play the victim here. Do you hear me?"

He yelled the words in her face. Nancy whimpered in fear and tried to cover her face with her hands. He placed the gun against the skin on her forehead. She felt its coldness through her body, then begged for her life.

"Please, don't, please."

The intruder panted then groaned angrily, speaking through gritted teeth. "I warned you, yet you didn't listen. Why wouldn't you listen, Nancy? Why did you have to go and ruin everything? Again?"

The finger lingered on the trigger and moved just as there was a loud knock, almost a hammering on the front door. Nancy's eyes sprang wide open. Someone was here. Was she saved?

"Nancy?"

Nancy recognized Agent Thomas's voice. Her heart leaped with hope. Could she be this lucky?

"Help!" she yelled. "Help me!"

The intruder's focus shifted to the door as Agent Thomas grabbed the handle but found it locked. Then she kept hammering on it.

"Nancy? Nancy?"

Nancy looked up at the intruder, and then she realized he wasn't paying attention; he was too worried about the threat coming from outside the door. She lifted her foot and kicked the gun out of his hand. The gun flew through the air, then landed on the tiles, where it slid toward the front door. Seeing this, the intruder glared down at her, then grabbed her around the throat.

"I'm gonna kill you… You…"

The pressure on her throat became tight, and Nancy struggled to breathe. It felt like an impossible task. The grip became tighter and what air she pulled in was so little it couldn't keep her conscious for much longer. Agent Thomas was still hammering at the door, hard, and soon kicking it. It would be a matter of seconds before she broke through.

But would she make it in time? Before the intruder managed to strangle her?

"H-help," she gurgled, but not much sound came out through her lips. She felt herself slip away, and the darkness surrounded her.

Please, help me, she tried to say. But it remained a thought in her trapped mind as she drifted away into deep oblivion.

Chapter 47

I KICKED in the door and blasted through it, gun raised. I could hear that Nancy was in distress on the other side, and as I came in, a person in a dark green hoodie stood above her, hands clasped around her throat, arms shaking.

"HEY!"

I stormed inside. Seeing me, the person let go of Nancy and let her sink to the wooden floors. Then he turned around and ran for the back door. I took off after him, but he was fast, and the screen door slammed behind him as he got away. I made it to the back porch, where I watched him run across the lawn, making it to the neighboring yard, jumping the fence. I grabbed my phone and called Merritt Island Police and gave them a description of the hoodie and how tall the intruder was. Then I hurried back to Nancy. I knelt beside her and felt for a pulse.

"Nancy, oh, dear God, Nancy. Are you there?"

My fingertips found a beating rhythm, and soon she moaned and opened her eyes.

"Nancy? Are you okay?"

She tried to sit up, and I helped her, supporting her back.

"Nancy? Are you all right? You're shaking!"

She nodded, then looked up at me, her eyes squinting. "Thank you, Agent Thomas. Thank you for coming, when…"

"Nancy, you've been hurt. I am going to take you to the hospital, come."

She shook me off, then tried to get up. "No, no. I don't want to go back there. Please. I'm fine; I just need to…"

She reached for a chair.

"Here. Let me help you," I said and lifted her so she could get into it. Nancy sat down, then hid her face between her hands.

"Look at me; I'm shaking," she said like she was just finally realizing what had happened.

"Nancy, I want you to try and focus here. Who was he?"

She shook her head. "I don't know. He just came in through the back door, and then he…he…"

"Did you see his face, Nancy? This is important."

"I…no, it all went by so fast…"

"Are you sure you didn't see any part of his face? Like a beard or the shape of his nose? Anything?"

"I…I don't know, okay. I was just passed out, and I can't…"

She began to cry. I grabbed her and pulled her into a hug. Her torso shook heavily, and her sobs became deep and desperate while I held her.

"Okay. Okay," I said. "Easy now. We'll find out who he was. Don't worry. Maybe you'll remember things later."

She nodded and sobbed while I held her. We sat like that for a long time, and I felt awful for her.

"I am so glad you were here," she finally said as the sobs died out. "You saved me, Eva Rae. You saved my life."

She coughed, then paused. "Why are you here?"

I smiled. "I came to talk to you. Let me get you a glass of water first. There's a lot we need to talk about."

Chapter 48

THE POLICE CARS ARRIVED, and they sent in the techs to look for any trace of the attacker. Nancy told her story to the responding officer, and then we were told to leave the living room while they worked. Patrols were searching for the guy in the green hoodie, and meanwhile, Nancy and I went to the kitchen and sat down. I found some ice cream in the freezer and took it out, then made us some coffee and served us both a bowl of mint chip. We sat down at the round table, eating it and drinking coffee, while officers walked in and out of the house to the sound of their scratching radios.

Nancy was getting the color back in her cheeks and beginning to calm down. I ate my ice cream while looking at her and the bruises on her neck. I really wanted to take her to the hospital and have someone take a look at it, but she refused. She said she was fine. She had been through worse.

I guessed she was right.

"There was something I needed to talk to you about," I said, breaking the silence after she had calmed down enough for me to bring it up.

She nodded, then wiped her fingers on a napkin. "I figured as much."

I leaned forward, trying to look into her eyes. She lifted her gaze and met mine. She seemed to be putting on a face.

"You said you had come here to talk to me, so…I assumed…"

I nodded. "We've had some news earlier today that I need to present to you. Something that…well, frankly, surprised me a little."

Nancy bit her lip.

"Okay?"

"The DNA we found in the shed," I said. I paused for effect, waiting for her to realize where I was going with this. She looked at me.

"We got the results back, and…it wasn't yours," I continued. "It wasn't a match."

Her body became stiff. Then she shook her head. "I don't really know what to say to that. What does it mean?"

I ate more of my ice cream. "It isn't good for our case. It doesn't look good at all right now. First, we have Mrs. Berkeley being killed, our star witness from both the night when you were kidnapped, and the night you were almost killed in the yard. And now this? If we have no DNA from the shed, we can't prove you were kept there."

"But…I was," she said.

"And are you sure about that? Do you remember anything?"

Nancy's eyes drifted. "I've started hypnotherapy with a therapist. Parts have been coming back to me."

"Okay, so like…what? What do you remember now?"

Nancy rubbed her hands together and looked down at them. Her shoulders came up. "It's…it's really hard to talk about right now. It's too painful. You have to remember; he was…my own husband."

"I understand, Nancy. But we need something to place you in that shed, or the prosecutor can't use it in the courtroom. And where does that leave us? You don't want Charles to go free, do you?"

She shook her head, staring at the table. "Of course not. I just…well it's hard, you know?"

I nodded and placed my hand on top of hers. "I know it is."

I glanced at the pictures on the wall behind her. They were all old ones of the children, school pictures and one of the son from scout camp. I recognized him from the hospital.

"Have they come around?" I asked and nodded toward the framed pictures.

She lifted her gaze and looked at them, then shook her head.

"They will," I said. "Eventually."

"I'm not sure," she said, sipping her coffee. "They believe in their dad's innocence. I can't blame them. He's all they've known for the past five years. They barely know who I am anymore."

"So, they haven't contacted you at all?"

"My son called right when his father was arrested, and it was all over the news. But I could tell it was still too hard for him. I asked him to come down for the weekend, but he wasn't sure he'd be able to make it. I call my daughter often, but she doesn't have time to talk. They're so busy, you know? At that age. So much going on."

"Of course," I said, not looking forward to that part of my children's lives. Right now, they were teenagers and really annoying most of the time, but I still told myself to enjoy every second because suddenly they'd be out of the house, and who knew when they'd come back to see me? If they were anything like me, they'd stay away as much as possible.

I sure hoped they weren't anything like me.

"It's just so hard when you don't really know who you are," Nancy said. "I don't remember much from the past five years, and that leaves me not really knowing who I am. Does that make any sense?"

"Sure."

"How do I expect my children to know who I am or to love me when I don't even know?"

"No, you're right. It's not an easy situation." I fiddled with the cup between my hands. I looked up. "It kind of reminds me of that movie. I don't recall its name. It's about this woman who gets cancer and runs away from her family because she doesn't want them to be hurt by having to watch her slowly deteriorating. And then when she's about to die, she finally tells them to call for her children, but they're angry with her and won't come at first. In the end, they forgive her just before she dies, and it's all sobs and cries. Have you seen it?"

Nancy nodded. "I know which one you mean. It's called *The Way You Were*. It was cute but not my favorite."

I stared at her, biting my lip. "I often wonder where I would go if I just could go anywhere—if I were to run away. Not that I could ever leave my children, but I think I might go to Alaska."

"For me, it's Key West. I have always loved the keys. The beaches, the snorkeling, the sunset festivals."

"The keys, huh? Yeah, I like it there too. Very hot, though."

"Agent Thomas?"

It was Detective Roberts. He had arrived from the sheriff's office, and I had promised to update him on what happened.

"Excuse me," I said to Nancy and got up.

"No worries," she said as I left.

"How is she?" Roberts asked as I came out on the other side of the door.

I smiled. "I think she's better than we give her credit for."

We walked to the living room where the techs were measuring up and dusting for prints.

"What do you mean by that?"

"I'm not sure yet," I said pensively. "I'll have to get back to you on that."

Chapter 49

THEN:

If you don't tell her, I will.

Ethan's words were nagging at her in the back of her mind. He kept telling her to talk to their mom about Billy—to tell her the truth. Yet Jade hadn't been able to, and Billy still came over often, eating dinner or helping their mom out with something. It felt like he was just always there.

Jade sat in her room, trying to find the courage. She closed her eyes and clenched her fists. She didn't want to do this. She really didn't. She knew her mom would be sad; she might even cry, and there was nothing worse in the world.

How am I even supposed to say it? How? And what afterward? Will she look at me differently? Will she think I started it? That I made him think I wanted him to do it? I did wear that dress at the party. He liked the dress, he said. If only I hadn't worn it? Maybe it's my own fault. He'll say it was anyway, and who will she believe? I did look at him and smile at him.

I liked him. I wanted him to like me too.

"No," Jade said and shook her head. She glared at her own reflection in the body-sized mirror covering her wall next to her bed. She barely recognized herself anymore. Her hair was greasy, and she was without makeup. She couldn't remember the last time she had put on even mascara. She didn't like to look at herself anymore. "It's a mistake. There is no way this can end well. It's his word against mine, and maybe…well, maybe I wanted it to happen."

Jade looked down at her fingers. She had bitten the nails down so far; there was barely anything left. The hoodie she was wearing smelled bad and needed to be washed. But she didn't want to take it off and had been sleeping in it as well.

She was a mess.

Please, don't make me do it! Can't we just leave it where it is and forget about it? No one needs to know.

Jade touched her stomach gently as a tear escaped her eye. It rolled slowly down her cheek till it landed on her upper lip, paving the way for a few more that followed. She didn't even bother to wipe them away. She stared at her reflection, wondering if her mother would ever look at her the same way after this. Would her brother? Would anything in life ever be good again?

Don't let him get away with it.

Her brother's words felt harsh. He didn't understand, did he? What it was like to fall in love with someone out of your reach, to want something to happen, and then when it did, it was just so wrong and not anything like what she wanted it to be. She could barely think about it, think about Billy, or the way he touched her that night. She had liked it when he kissed her because she liked him. But what followed made her feel dirty and made her angry with herself. Why had she wanted him to touch her? Why had she worn that dress? Why had she said yes to that stupid massage? Didn't that mean she had said yes to what followed? Just because she didn't like it? She had still started it. And worst of all, she hadn't said no. She hadn't told him not to touch her the way he did. She had just remained completely still, thinking it would soon be over. Thinking that if she let him have his way, it'd be over faster, and he'd be happy. She wanted him to be happy. She wanted to give herself to him and give him what he desired even if it didn't feel good, especially not when he pressed her head down and held her in a tight grip. Especially not when he had put a hand over her mouth and put his weight on top of her, or when he had been inside of her and had kept turning her head away so she couldn't look at him.

Why isn't he kissing me? she had thought while he held her head down. *If he likes me so much?*

Jade rose to her feet and wiped her tears away with her sleeve. No, her brother was right. Her mother needed to know. It didn't matter what she thought afterward. It had to be said.

Now, before she changed her mind.

Part III

ONE WEEK LATER

Chapter 50

I WALKED INTO ROBERTS' office, then closed the door behind me. He looked up from his computer screen.

"Agent Thomas? I didn't expect you here today?"

I threw the file I had under my arm on his desk, then sat in the chair across from him. "Do you have any decent coffee in this place? I'll be here for a little while. We have a lot to talk about."

His face lit up. "Sure. Let me get you a cup."

He left and returned with a plastic cup of coffee that he placed on the desk in front of me. I tasted it. It was as awful as I could expect, but it would have to do. I had been up most of the night, going over the case in my mind, pondering it, and needed a caffeine boost to get me going.

"So, what's going on?" he asked as he sat back down. "You seem…animated?"

I didn't want to tell him that I had thrown up all morning and therefore felt everything but that.

"I think I found something important."

"Really?"

"You know how I told you at Nancy Henry's house that I believed she was doing better than we thought?"

"Sure."

"I had a hunch back then. You told me it wasn't her DNA we had found in the shed, and I started to wonder about that a lot. Still, she claimed she had been there, and she said she remembered things now, after being in hypnotherapy. But I think she's lying."

Roberts leaned forward and placed his hands on the desk.

"And why is that?"

"I tested her afterward. I asked her about a movie, *The Way You Were*, and she told me she had seen it."

A crease appeared between Roberts' eyes.

"The movie was released two years ago," I continued.

He tipped his head. "Okay. But maybe she has seen it after she came back. It could be on Netflix."

"I know. It's not proof, but it made me very suspicious. So, I asked her where she might go if she had to hide somewhere from those she loved like the woman in the movie. I said I'd go to Alaska, which is also a lie because I could never stand the cold, but nevertheless, she said Key West."

"I think I see where you're going with this."

I placed a hand on the file on his desk. "I have a relative who is really good with computers. I know the sheriff's office doesn't have the manpower or time to do something like this, so I had him do it. I had him search surveillance cameras from Key West from the past five years and run a face recognition program, and guess what?"

I opened the file and placed a series of photos in front of him. Most of them were from ATMs or bar security cameras. He looked at them, and I pointed at the woman in one.

"Recognize someone?"

Roberts grabbed the photo and lifted it to see better.

"I'll be…"

"Taken three years ago. The hair is slightly different, but she sure doesn't look like she's being held kidnapped in a shed, now does she? She's got a pretty good tan going and is smiling at that man right there."

Roberts nodded. He looked up at me, appalled. "But why? Why would she lie?"

I leaned back. "That's what I don't know. My guess is we need to go back to that night five years ago when she disappeared. When we figure out what really happened that night, we'll know why."

"And exactly how do you suggest that we do that? I don't think Nancy will talk much, and neither will Charles, or he would have done that by now."

I placed a hand on my stomach and sighed.

"That's the other thing I don't know."

Chapter 51

THE LONELINESS in the big house felt crushing. It used to be so vibrating with life, with the sounds of the children fighting or playing, little feet tiptoeing across the floor. Nancy stood by the window and remembered Tinkerbell's first steps by the door, when she had let go of the wall and walked out into the living room without holding on, beginning her journey out into the big and scary world.

How she missed them both. How deeply she longed for them.

Nancy was going to do an interview later in the afternoon with the guy who was supposed to do the screenplay for the movie they were making about her. But she really didn't want to. They were coming to her house all the way from Hollywood, but now she most of all wanted to call them back and tell them she couldn't do it.

Except she couldn't. She had accepted the money. And it was a lot —enough for her not to have to work for years. Yet she wasn't sure she was ready to talk about the things that happened. Did she have the story prepared? She'd have to be extremely careful with the details. Nothing could contradict the things she had told the police or the reporters in her many interviews.

Nancy shivered slightly and wondered if she would be able to pull it off without mistakes. It wasn't as easy being a liar as you'd think.

Her phone buzzed in the kitchen, and she went out to look at it. Another text had come in:

I HATE YOU.

Nancy stared at the text, then deleted it. A second later, another one came:

I HOPE YOU DIE.

Nancy grabbed an apple and took a bite from it. She had been getting a lot of texts like these lately. They kept coming. She tried her best to ignore them, but it was hard to. Would this ever end?

She deleted this text as well, then put the phone down, placing the screen downward against the counter. Her stomach was in knots, and she felt like she could cry if she allowed herself to. She was pretending like the words didn't get to her, but the truth was, they did. They hurt her deeply and scared her too.

The phone buzzed again.

Nancy stared at it, eating her apple. She didn't want to look at the screen. She knew it was probably another one of those nasty texts, and she didn't want to read it. She bit into the apple and finished it, then threw away the remains. The phone buzzed again, and the sound made her jump.

Heart in her throat, she caved in. She grabbed the phone and looked at the screen.

I WILL BE BACK FOR YOU

She put the phone down, heart throbbing in her chest. She stared at the phone like it would jump up and bite her, then decided it was time to bite back. She took the phone and wrote a text:

OKAY. YOU WIN. I'LL LEAVE IF THAT'S WHAT IT TAKES. LET'S MEET AND TALK. SOMEWHERE PUBLIC.

Feeling like her heart would explode, she put the phone down and waited for the response. It took longer than she had expected. It came with a time and a place. She texted back:

NO GUNS THIS TIME.

Chapter 52

A THUNDERSTORM HIT us just as we drove across the bridge toward Merritt Island, and it rained so hard I had to slow down the minivan. I was following Detective Roberts in his police cruiser, driving ahead of me, while speculating about all this new information. If Nancy had been in Key West all this time, then why did she lie? Why did she tell us she had been held captive in that shed? Charles was in custody, waiting for his trial for having kidnapped her. Did this mean he had never laid a hand on her? Was he innocent?

Someone cut in front of me, and I had to hit the brakes. I slammed a hand on the steering wheel.

"You've got to be kidding me."

The car in front of me slowed down, and I lost sight of Roberts' cruiser. I tried to surpass it on the other side, but a pick-up truck blocked me. I slowed down with a deep sigh while the rain hammered my windshield, and my wipers fought to keep up.

I can't believe she tricked us. She tricked everyone into believing her husband did this to her, and then she was just down there, in the Keys, having a blast?

"But Mrs. Berkeley saw Charles run away from the yard when

someone tried to kill her?" I mumbled. "She was so certain it was him?"

We finally reached the exit to Merritt Island, and I turned, getting away from the slow car in front of me. The rain was still coming down hard, but I sped up and entered South Tropical Trail.

"And someone did try to kill her; we know that much," I said as I rushed up the narrow road, cutting through south Merritt Island, where the million-dollar mansions with Roman columns and lion statues outside their gates towered on my left side, overlooking the Banana River.

"I was there the day someone tried to kill her in her house. I saw him run across the lawn. So it can't be Charles. Could it be someone he hired?"

The thought seemed plausible, yet I couldn't see why he would. If he was innocent? And what about Mrs. Berkeley? Who killed her? Could it have been Nancy? But why would she kill her? If the goal was to get Charles convicted, then she was vital to getting that done. Without her, there was barely a case. She was the most important witness.

Why get rid of her?

I shook my head as the rain died down slightly, and I turned onto Old Settlement Road. The Georgianna Methodist church on my left side sat there looking like nothing had changed in the neighborhood for the past hundred years, and probably never would. There was something eerie about that old wooden building, especially when it rained. I couldn't say what it was; maybe it was just how I felt about this street with all its Spanish moss dangling from the trees and the expensive houses. I think it was the quietness that got to me.

I stopped the car in front of the Henrys' house and got out, then ran to the porch, where Roberts had already made it up the stairs. He knocked on the door.

"Nancy Henry?"

I could tell by the sound of his voice that he was agitated. I couldn't blame him. I was too. None of us liked to be taken for fools. Nancy had some serious explaining to do.

He knocked again, and then again.

"Police! Open up!"

"I don't think she's home," I said. "The car is gone."

He growled and rubbed his wet hair. "Dang it. You think she realized we were coming and took off?"

I peeked in through the window, covering my eyes with my hands. "I'm not sure. I don't see how she could have known…" I paused as my eyes fell on something inside the house. A case left open on the kitchen counter.

On the outside, it said *Smith & Wesson*.

Chapter 53

THEN:

Jade walked down the hallway, taking cautious steps. She was wondering how to open the conversation she was about to have with her mother. What would she say? How did you tell something like this?

Her stomach was in knots just from thinking about it.

He's a pig and needs to be punished for what he has done. You're the one who is the victim here. Not him. He's the grown-up and should know better.

Those were Ethan's words, and she kept repeating them to herself, but she wasn't sure she believed them. She kept making excuses for Billy—telling herself that she wanted it to happen, that she had led him on. She hadn't said no, so how would he know she didn't want it to happen? And what if she did want him to do those things?

You're sixteen, Jade. He's forty. It's criminal.

But she had liked his attention and even liked it when he touched her. Wasn't it her own fault, then?

It was confusing.

"Mom, I need to talk to you..." she mumbled as she came closer to the door to her mother's bedroom. She slowed her pace, trying to buy herself time to think. Everything felt so foggy in her brain, and it was hard to find the words.

"Mom," she continued to mumble, "there's something I need to tell you, and you won't like it. Please, don't be mad. Please."

Jade shook her head. No, she couldn't start like that. It would freak her mother out before she even got to the important stuff.

"Mom, you know Billy, right...?"

She whispered it to herself, trying to get the words across her lips, thinking it would make it easier, but it didn't. Hearing herself say it made it even worse.

What would her mom think of her? Would she look at her differently? Would she ever see her as her little girl again?

"Mom, you know how Billy is..."

She took in a deep breath, then lifted her hand to place it on the doorknob to her mother's room. She pushed the door open and stepped in, trying to shove that sense of doom and dread back into her stomach. She took one step into the bedroom when she saw them.

Her mother was sitting on top of him.

As she saw Jade, she pulled the covers up to cover her body.

"Sweetie? I didn't even know you were home?"

Eyes wide, Jade stared at her mother, her very naked mother, and then at the guy in the bed. The very naked guy in the bed.

She could barely breathe.

"Honey? It's not...I mean..." her mother jumped down from the bed, and from Billy, then walked toward her, holding out a hand.

"Honey?"

Jade shook her head and took a step back, heart throbbing in her chest. Seeing Billy's naked body again took her straight back to that night in her room, the night of the party, and she felt like she had to throw up.

Jade turned around, then stormed out of the bedroom, holding a hand over her mouth, bile biting in her throat.

Chapter 54

NANCY LOOKED NERVOUSLY AROUND HER. The gun was tucked away safely in her purse. She had bought it after the last attack on her life, not wanting to live unarmed any longer. It was time to fight back if it came to that. She was done being shamed, being told what to do, and living in fear.

It was time to take back her life.

She walked up to the restaurant's patio overlooking the water, then sat down at a table that had been covered by the rain from part of the roof that was hanging out. The sun had come out now that the thunderstorm was over, and her chair was only slightly wet. She didn't really care.

A waitress came to her and asked if she could get her anything. Nancy told her she was waiting for someone, but she could start with a glass of Chardonnay.

The waitress looked cute when she smiled. She had dimples on each cheek, and her brown eyes grew narrow.

"Of course. Say…aren't you…?"

Nancy nodded. "Yes, that's me."

"I thought I had seen you before," she said. "I can't believe what that pig did to you. Good for you that he's now in jail. Let's hope they keep him there."

Nancy nodded with a smile. "Let's."

Nancy sighed as the waitress disappeared, then glared out over the water. It was so still now since it had just rained. The water was glassy, and the wind had completely died down. A fish jumped up and splashed down again.

To be a fish in the water, she thought. *Just swimming along. Without a single care in the world.*

The Chardonnay arrived, and she sipped the glass, then looked at her watch. She was early, and there were still a few minutes till they were supposed to meet. Her heart was pounding loudly, and she put a hand on her chest as if she could calm it down that way. The wine made her calmer and more determined, but it didn't make her heart beat slower.

She was scared, and rightfully so.

But she didn't want to be afraid anymore. She didn't want to live like this. Not anymore. It had to end here.

Today.

She put the purse on the chair next to her, then reached inside and felt for the gun. She could easily pull it out when needed.

She sighed, relieved, thinking that she hated to do this more than anything, but it had to be done. Something had to be done. She couldn't live her life like this, in a constant state of fear. She had managed to take her life back, and there was no way she was going to return to where she came from.

No way.

A small breeze came from the water and lifted her hair lightly. It felt good in the muggy heat. Normally, she'd sit inside on a day like today, but she wanted to meet outside. She couldn't risk anyone overhearing their conversation and telling the media. At the same time, she needed it to be a public place to feel safe.

No one would try to murder her in public. At her house, yes, when she was all alone. But not here.

And no one would expect her to try and murder them either. It was going to be the perfect surprise.

Chapter 55

"WE NEED to figure out where she is," I said and rubbed my forehead. It felt clammy as the sun scorched down on us, standing out on the Henrys' porch. "If she took a gun, there's no telling what she's up to. I hardly think she went for a yoga class."

"Couldn't she just have taken it for protection?" Roberts asked. "She might have been scared, and can you blame her? Someone definitely is trying to kill her. She was attacked twice."

I bit my lip while pondering. "Maybe you're right. I just don't have a good feeling about this. Something is off."

"I'll tell dispatch to put out a search for her," Roberts said and walked back to the cruiser. "We need to bring her in for questioning. Maybe a patrol car will spot her somewhere. Give me a sec."

I stared at Roberts as he disappeared inside the car, then lifted my gaze to look at the house across the street. Police tape was still wrapped around the porch. I could still see the image of Mrs. Berkeley's dead body in the living room, and those eyes, and once again, I wondered what they had seen in those last moments. Why did she have to be killed? Was there something she hadn't told us? I had followed the sheriff's team's investigation closely, but nothing so far helped point me in the direction of the murderer. Whoever it was had been very careful.

I turned to look at the beautiful mansion in front of me with the heart wreath on the door. Nancy had been gone for five years. Someone had been after her that night and pulled her back inside the house when she tried to get away. Was it that same person who had attacked her the other night when I came to her house? Was it the same person who had tried to shoot her that night outside the guest cottage? She had told us it was Charles, and Mrs. Berkeley had confirmed that she saw him too, at least she was *pretty sure* it was him.

"What if it wasn't him?" I said out loud as Roberts came out of the cruiser and walked back up toward me.

"What's that?" he asked.

"What if it is the same guy that attacked her that night I stopped by, and what if she's agreed to meet him right now?"

Roberts narrowed his eyes. "That sounds a little far-fetched. Why would she agree to meet with him? Where is all this coming from?"

A car drove up while we still stood on the porch. Two men got out and approached us. They gave us a suspicious look when seeing the police cruiser.

"Yes?" I asked and faced them. "Can we help you?"

"We're here to visit Nancy Henry. This is her place, right?" the first one said. He was only slightly taller than me, skinny, and wore a small scarf. He looked like an artist. The other was more businesslike, wearing a suit but no tie.

"It is," I said. "Who are you?"

"I'm her agent," the one in the suit said. "I have come down from New York; Bellman here flew in from L.A. this morning. We're supposed to meet Nancy here at her house. Is she here?"

"You came in vain," I said. "She's not home."

"I'll try her cell," the suit guy said and tapped on his phone. "This must be some misunderstanding."

"We are trying to locate her too," Roberts said and showed them his badge. "We need to bring her in for questioning."

"Questioning? But…but she's supposed to talk to us," the guy with the scarf, Bellman, said. "We have an exclusive deal. She's telling us her story of being kidnapped for five whole years by her husband. For the movie script we're making."

I shrugged. "I'm not sure she'll be able to talk today. We're taking her in. And you might want to wait with the script until we figure out what really happened. Just a piece of advice here."

He looked appalled. "But… but… this is…"

"I can't reach her; she's not picking up, and it goes straight to voicemail," the suit guy said, coming back toward us. His cheeks were blushing, probably from the heat and the embarrassment. "I left her a couple of messages."

"Maybe you should go to your hotel and wait to see what happens next," I said. "Hopefully, we'll know the truth soon."

"So, you're basically telling me that she's been lying? Is that it?" the man with the scarf asked.

"I can't tell you that as it is right now since we don't know for sure, and it's an ongoing investigation," I said.

"You're kidding me, right? Tell me you're joking here."

"I am afraid not."

"Do you have any idea how much money the studio has paid for this deal?" the man with the scarf said, pointing his finger at me like it was somehow my fault. His nostrils flared, and his tone told me he was trying to hold it back but failing. "She better have that story for us."

The men both shook their heads like, somehow, we were the ones who had been lying to them. I did my best to ignore them. The suit guy grabbed the other one by the arm.

"We're not getting anything out of standing here. Let's go back."

The one with the scarf complained loudly. As they walked to the car, he gesticulated wildly. Once they had left, I turned to Roberts.

"Now, I am certain something is wrong. Nancy has been so excited for this movie deal to happen," I said. "There is no way she would have missed that freely. Something came up suddenly, and it made her take her gun."

Roberts nodded pensively. "I see what you mean. I can try and have them trace her phone."

"It sounds like it's turned off," I said. "Besides, it takes too long. We need to find her now—before something awful happens. I have this sense of deep dread. If we don't find her in time, something terrible is going to happen. She might end up getting killed or do something she'll regret later."

Chapter 56

HER GLASS of white wine was almost empty, and she felt the sweat start to tickle her upper lip. She was slightly tipsy, but not enough not to keep her head clear should the situation escalate.

She felt his presence as he walked up behind her. She recognized the sound of his steps, and her heart dropped.

"Sit down," she said.

He did as she told him to. His jaws were clenched, and he spoke through gritted teeth. His tone was flat, yet she could sense the sizzling anger underneath it. "I told you never to come back. Why did you?"

She glanced at her purse on the chair next to her and placed her hand close to it, making sure she could reach inside quickly should it be needed. Her stomach became a small hard ball.

"Do you want anything to eat?"

He shook his head.

"I'll pay."

"I don't want anything from you, and you know it."

Nancy cleared her throat, then drank the rest of her wine quickly.

"So, why did you?" he asked. "Why did you come back?"

She glared at him, and their eyes met across the table. Her heart melted when looking into them. She had missed those eyes for such a long time, and she had loved them so deeply.

"I wanted my life back," she said, trying to hide that she was about to cry. Sitting there in front of him again was harder than she had expected it to be. She had thought she could keep her emotions out of this meeting, but she still felt herself tear up, then pressed it back. This was no time for strong emotions, no matter how long they had been suppressed. In him, there clearly weren't the same feelings left. The anger was so deep and so harmful, there was no love in his eyes.

"I thought it was time."

"It wasn't your decision to make," he said.

She shrugged and pretended that his cold tone didn't make her want to cry. "It's still my life."

"Why are you lying to everyone?" he asked. His shoulders came down slightly. Was he easing up on her? Maybe all hope wasn't lost?

"I came here today to ask you to stop attacking me," she said.

"I thought you said you'd leave. That's why I came."

She nodded. "I know. I know. But the thing is, you need to stop what you're doing. Stop threatening me and stop attacking me, or I'll have to make you."

That made him pull into a smile. "How? I'd like to see you do that."

Nancy looked at his uniform and the badge glistening in the sun. He looked so handsome. He always did, but seeing him in uniform was always special. She reached out her hand across the table to touch his. He pulled his away.

"Don't."

She looked down, embarrassed. "I'm sorry. Old habit."

"What is it you want?" he asked. "I have to get back to work."

"What do you want?" she asked.

He leaned forward, and for a second, she thought she saw a shadow of something she mistook for care in his eyes. But it was a mistake. He looked into her eyes, his blazing with anger.

"I want you gone. I never ever want to see your ugly face around here again. Do you hear me?"

She felt tears well up in her eyes, but the hurt was soon replaced with anger. She was sick of his threats and his demeaning manner. It was about time she showed him who he was dealing with. She wanted him to regret what he had done to her. She wanted him to be in pain, the same kind of pain she had been through.

Without hesitation, Nancy reached into her purse and pulled out her gun.

Chapter 57

THEN:

"Sweetie?"

Jade kept walking down the hallway. Her mother came bursting out of the bedroom, a shirt half put on.

"Honey?"

Jade could hardly breathe. She didn't know what to do, what to say to her, and she just wanted her to go away. She felt sick to her stomach.

"Please, wait."

Jade finally stopped. She was leaning on the wall, still standing with her back turned to her mother.

"Please. Hear me out, will you?"

She swallowed the bile in her throat.

"Talk to me. Please. Turn around?"

Her mother placed a hand on her shoulder. Jade shivered at the touch. Knowing where those hands had been last, what—who—they had touched.

"Will you look at me?"

She pulled at her shoulder, and Jade finally turned to face her. Her mother smiled insecurely.

"Listen, sweetie…sometimes in a marriage…well, you know how much your father has been gone and…"

Jade couldn't stand to look at her. She just wanted to leave, to go to her room and crawl under the covers, where she'd hide for the rest of her life.

"Well, it's been hard on me. I don't expect you to understand, but I am lonely and well…you know how Billy has been there for me, and I think that we might…I don't know."

Jade lifted her eyes and met those of her mother's.

"You've…fallen in love?"

Her mother smiled again softly. "I don't know. Maybe?"

There was a light in her mother's eyes that Jade had never seen before. Could she really be in love with Billy? And if so, would Jade be able to destroy that? Now that her mother was finally happy? She had heard her crying at night for years. She had seen her on her bed, crying of loneliness.

She couldn't do that to her.

"Anyway, honey. I just…I need some time to think about what I want, okay? So, could I ask you to do me a favor?"

"A favor?"

Both hands landed on her shoulders. "Yes. A huge one. Please, don't tell your dad. It will only break his heart, and we don't want that. I need time to figure out what I want and what my next move will be. But until then, let's keep it between us, okay?"

Jade stared at her, heart throbbing in her throat. Her mom needed to figure out what she wanted? Did that mean that Billy could end up becoming her stepdad?

"Okay? Do we have a deal? And don't tell your brother either. Let's keep this between us, okay? A little secret between us girls. Okay?"

Jade could barely breathe. It was like everything in her throat suddenly became tight. When she finally spoke, it sounded hoarse and forced.

"O-okay."

Her mom leaned over and kissed her on the cheek. She smelled like him, and Jade felt like she had to throw up.

"Thank you, honey. I owe you one." She was about to walk away when she stopped herself. "Say, what did you want to talk to me about?"

"What do you mean?"

"You came to my room to talk to me about something, right?"

"Oh, that? I don't…it wasn't important."

Her mother tilted her head. "Are you sure? Whatever it is, you're sure to get a yes from me. I owe you one, a big one. So, once you think of it, come find me, okay?"

"Okay."

Her mother winked at her, then placed a finger on her own lips before she disappeared back inside the bedroom, where Jade could hear her laugh at something Billy said. Jade couldn't remember ever hearing her mother laugh quite like that.

Chapter 58

HALF AN HOUR LATER, we parked the cars behind Grills Riverside Restaurant. I got out and went up to Roberts, who took in the building next to him by the still Indian River.

"What are we doing here? I don't assume we're here because you're hungry?" he asked.

"Funny," I said without smiling.

"So, what makes you think she came here?"

I grabbed my phone and showed him the display, then tapped. A picture popped up. "Six minutes ago, this girl posted this picture on Instagram using the tag #JusticeforNancyHenry."

Roberts took the phone out of my hand and looked at it, squinting his eyes. "She's a waitress?"

I nodded. "And who do you see in the background? Sitting by the table outside on the deck, enjoying a glass of white wine?"

"Nancy Henry," he said.

"Exactly. The waitress took this picture and posted it under the caption MY PLEASURE TO SERVE THIS GREAT WOMAN TODAY, followed by some strong-arm emojis. Lots of women see themselves in Nancy Henry and want to see her succeed in getting her husband convicted, maybe even get the death penalty for what he did to her. It makes it hard for her to go anywhere unnoticed."

Roberts nodded and handed me back the phone. "I'm impressed, Agent Thomas. Very impressed."

"As you should be," I said with a smirk. "I am quite the savage when it comes to…"

I didn't get to finish the sentence. That's when the shot echoed through the air.

Roberts and I ducked down behind the cruiser, then shared a look, both reaching for our weapons, while Roberts called for assistance.

Screams emerged from inside the restaurant, and soon people were rushing out, faces torn in fear.

I signaled Roberts, and we went in, guns drawn, hearts in our throats, terrified of what we were going to find.

I signaled him that I would go out on the porch while he went inside the restaurant, yelling *police* as the remaining guests screamed at the sight of his gun and him waving his badge. Meanwhile, I walked out on the wooden deck, where I soon spotted Nancy sitting at a table, gun still in her hand.

Alone.

I walked closer, still pointing my gun at her.

"Nancy?"

She didn't move. I came closer and went up on her side.

"Nancy, it's Eva Rae. I need you to put down the gun. Can you do that for me?"

As I came up on her side, I realized her hand with the gun was shaking heavily, and she was crying. Tears were rolling down her cheeks. Her eyes were staring blankly into the vast space in front of her, and I realized someone had been sitting there. The chair was tipped over, probably when—whoever it was—had pushed it back and run away.

Running for his life.

"Nancy?" I said. "Please put down the gun."

She shook her head, then looked up at me, her face wet from tears.

"He doesn't love me anymore, Eva Rae. I thought when he saw me, when we faced one another like this, he might remember that he loved me once. But he doesn't. He wants to see me dead."

"I really want to talk to you about this, Nancy, but right now, I need you to put that gun down. Please."

I placed a hand gently on her arm, then moved closer to the gun, hoping I might snatch it from her hand. My heart was throbbing loudly in my chest as I reached out for the gun, but just as I was about to grab it, she pulled it away from me, then turned it toward herself, placing it on her forehead, pressing it hard against the skin.

"Maybe I should just give them all what they want."

I recoiled.

"No, Nancy. No!"

Chapter 59

HER FINGER SHOOK on the trigger while I stared in terror. She closed her eyes and moved the finger, tears rolling down her cheeks.

Then, she stopped.

Her finger didn't move anymore. Her face became torn in pain. The gun came down slowly and landed on the table in front of her, where I managed to grab it while Nancy hid her face between her hands. She looked shrunken, suddenly like a little girl. Seeing this brought a lump to my throat. Nancy shook from violent sobs, but no sound escaped. Her mouth was open, her torso in spasms.

Roberts came up behind me, and I handed him Nancy's gun discreetly, then knelt next to her, biting back my own tears.

"Nancy, please. Tell us. Who is he?"

But she was lost now. Lost in her own tears and grief. She didn't hear my words, and instead, I held her in my arms while she cried.

A patrol car arrived, and they took Nancy away. The gun was secured in a bag while they searched for the bullet. It was found lodged into the wooden fence behind the chair of whoever had been with Nancy. I stared at the location, then looked at Roberts.

"Look at the angle. She didn't even try to hit him."

"What are you saying?"

"It was a warning shot."

Roberts nodded. "I think you might be right. They were sitting across from one another. If she wanted to kill him, she could have done so easily."

I nodded.

"So, what do you think it was about?" Roberts asked. "If it wasn't a murder attempt?"

I shrugged. "Scare him off? She said something about him not loving her anymore when I got here. That she had believed he would remember how much he loved her if they met here. I say it was the same guy that tried to kill her both in the yard and in the house and maybe even before she was pulled out of Sykes Creek. Maybe it was even the same guy back five years ago?"

"But she thought he loved her?" Roberts asked, concerned. "Doesn't really sound like love to me."

"It can't be Charles. That much is clear."

Roberts rubbed his chin. "I don't really know what is up and down in this case anymore."

"Hopefully, Nancy can tell us more once we interrogate her when she has calmed down," I said, walking to my minivan. An investigative team from the sheriff's office had arrived and taken over the interviews of guests and the waitress. I grabbed my keys from my pocket, then unlocked the car.

"She said he was wearing a uniform, by the way," Roberts said.

I stopped. "Who did?"

"The guy she was talking to before she decided to try and shoot at him. The waitress told me this, you know, your little friend from Instagram. I didn't want to say anything while we were up there where everyone could hear it."

I wrinkled my forehead. "What kind of uniform?"

"Green. Like the ones they wear at the sheriff's office. Her words, not mine."

My eyes grew wide. "You're kidding me? So, he's one of your guys?"

Roberts exhaled. "Just when we didn't think it could get any more complicated, right?"

He could say that again.

Chapter 60

IT DIDN'T MAKE me feel good about myself, but it had to be done as quickly as possible. Nancy was in no state to talk, but we had to try and get her to while the event was still fresh in her mind.

They had put her in an interrogation room at the sheriff's office, her hands cuffed. She was leaning her forehead on her hands, hiding her face as Roberts and I entered.

I took a deep breath, preparing myself for this being tough on all of us. Nancy was a mess, and it broke my heart to see her like this.

Yet we had a lot of questions that needed answers.

"Nancy?" I said as I sat down in front of her.

Roberts placed a file on the desk, then sat down as well.

Nancy stifled a sob, and her head jerked up. She glared at us, eyes red and filled with yet unshed tears.

I tried to smile. Then I opened the file. Nancy stared at the pictures I brought out and placed in front of her. The look in her eyes made me certain she knew it was over. The lie had been revealed.

I folded my hands on the table. "Nancy. We know you weren't in that shed. These pictures were taken in Key West three years ago."

I tapped my finger on her face in the photos and sent my dad a grateful thought. Without his help, we wouldn't have been able to find these so fast. He was a true magician.

"You don't look much like you're being held against your will there," Roberts said.

"Plus, the DNA we found in the shed didn't match yours, but you already know that."

Roberts tapped his fingers on the table. "It was actually animal DNA. Someone had kept a dog there tied up recently. Despicable, but it had nothing to do with you, did it?"

Nancy's shoulders sagged.

I exhaled. "Why did you lie?"

Nancy's big eyes landed on me.

"Was it to get Charles in trouble?" Roberts asked, his tone showing he was getting annoyed. "So you could get rid of him?"

She took me in, her gaze sweeping rapidly over me.

"Help us out a little, Nancy," I said. "We want to understand. I think you have a good reason for all this, but you need to tell us about it. Otherwise, I can't keep defending you. It doesn't look good for you."

"Especially not after today," Roberts said. "Firing a weapon in a crowded restaurant. Are you crazy? Innocents could have been hurt."

"But no one was hurt," Nancy said, her voice not much more than a whisper. "No one was hurt. I made sure of that."

Finally, she was talking. I leaned forward.

"Exactly. I don't think you wanted to kill him. So help us help you. But you have to talk to us. Who is he?"

Nancy clammed up. She leaned back in her chair.

"Come on, Nancy," I said. "We're trying to help you. This guy tried to kill you several times. Was he the same person that threw you in the water?"

Her eyes became distant, and she looked down, avoiding our eyes.

"Nancy, dang it," I said. "We can't help you if you don't talk to us."

"I want my lawyer," she said with a small whisper.

"Who is trying to hurt you, Nancy?" I asked, at my wit's end. Why wouldn't she just tell us? Didn't she understand how important it was that we stopped him?

"Why are you protecting him?" I continued. "You think he still loves you? It sure doesn't look like it. He tried to kill you three times. Three times, Nancy. Come on. No one is stupid enough to protect a guy like that? After all that he has done to you?"

She lifted her gaze, her stare piercing into my eyes.

"I want to talk to my lawyer. Please."

Chapter 61

THEN:

"Sweetie?"

Jade's dad poked his head in through the door to her room. She felt a chill run rapidly down her spine as she looked up from her bed, and her eyes met his. She sat up, pulling her knees up under her chin. He came in and sat down on the edge of her bed. A frown made deep crease lines in his forehead and around his eyes.

"Honey? Is everything okay?"

She nodded, biting her cheek. He scrutinized her.

"Are you sure?"

She nodded again, her eyes avoiding his, looking at the bedcover instead, then ran a hand across it like she was trying to straighten it.

"Jade? Look at me."

She swallowed, then lifted her gaze and looked into his eyes. It almost made her lose it. She loved her father more than anyone in the world. Carrying this secret—both of them—threatened to destroy her.

"You don't look okay to me. Ever since I came home, I feel you've been avoiding me, and you don't hang out with your brother either. You just sit up here, watching whatever it is you watch on that computer."

She scoffed. "Anime."

He nodded with a grin. "Yes, that awful Japanese stuff. Good to see that you're still into that. I never understood the fascination with it, but at least that's more like you. You, barely talking to me or the rest of the family isn't."

He paused to see her reaction, and she shrugged it off.

"I'm fine, really."

He tilted his head. Jade felt like screaming. She had never kept secrets from her father. Never. He was the one she could confide in when her mother wouldn't understand. He would protect her if she did something wrong and feared her mother's wrath.

"Go easy on her. She didn't mean anything bad. Try to put yourself in her place?"

He would say stuff like that to make her mother back off. He was her closest ally, even closer than Ethan. They shared a different bond, a father-daughter bond that she had believed was unbreakable. But now she was keeping secrets from him, deep, ugly secrets, bad secrets, dirty and disgusting ones, and she couldn't tell him about it—even though he was the one she wanted to tell the most.

But you can't. It'll devastate him.

He pushed her lovingly with an elbow. "Come on. I'm not falling for that. I know my daughter. Talk to me."

"It's nothing, Dad, really. Just...well, the usual stuff with my friends and...you know. School."

She didn't look at him when she spoke. She tried to, but she simply couldn't. He'd know she was lying. He'd be able to see it in her eyes. He knew her too well.

Lying to his face was the hardest thing she ever had to do. It broke her heart, shattered it to pieces.

Her dad nodded. "Okay. I know it's a tough age right now. It'll pass. It'll get better. I promise. And remember that friends come and go, while family is forever. We will always be here for you. And that goes for all of us, even your mother."

With that, he pulled her into a hug and kissed her forehead, while Jade could barely breathe. She closed her eyes and suppressed her desire to scream while wondering if it was possible to drown without being actually sunk into water.

Chapter 62

WE DIDN'T GET another word out of Nancy. She asked for her lawyer, and that was the end of her talking to us. I didn't understand why. I had tried to tell her that I was on her side, that I just wanted to find the guy who had been trying to kill her but little did it help. In the end, right before her lawyer arrived, she wouldn't even look at me anymore.

I went with Roberts to Firehouse Subs not far from the sheriff's office, and we grabbed a sandwich. I was starving and ate the whole thing in the car on our way back.

"I can't stop thinking about the uniform," I said, chewing the pastrami. "We need to tread carefully if he's one of your guys."

"I haven't told a soul so far," he said. "But I did ask dispatch to show me the location of all of our patrol cars at the time the shot was fired. None of them were near the restaurant."

"Really?" I said.

He nodded. "I'm not sure he's one of ours."

"That's odd," I said and took another bite of my sandwich. "Could he have been off duty? Maybe on his way home? Perhaps driving his private car?"

Roberts nodded and took a turn. "It's possible. But that doesn't make it easier to locate who he is."

Roberts parked the cruiser in front of the sheriff's office, and I finished my food, then washed it down with my Sprite. I didn't used to be a Sprite drinker, but since I got pregnant, it was all that could keep my nausea at bay.

"We need to deal with the elephant in the room," Roberts said.

I exhaled and finished my soda. "I know. I've been trying not to talk about it. But you're right."

Roberts got out. I followed and threw away my drink and paper in the garbage can outside. I followed him inside, then showed my ID to the guard. As we walked down the hallway, Roberts turned to me.

"We both know he is innocent. I have already told them to let him go."

"You did what? You let Charles go? Why?"

Roberts gave me a look. "Eh…Because he's innocent."

"Shoot. I wanted to have a last go at him. I wanted to see if we could get anything out of him. I mean, he must know more than what he is telling us."

"You don't think he would have told us by now?" Roberts said. "We interrogated him countless times about that night five years ago, and he sticks with his story. He came home and found there had been an intrusion. When he realized that Nancy was gone, he called the police."

I shook my head, annoyed. I wasn't ready to let him go yet. "There's got to be more to it than that. I have a feeling he is hiding something from us."

Roberts frowned. "Why? Don't you think he would have told us everything if it would help keep him out of jail? He was facing death row."

I stopped, then looked at him pensively. "But what if it wouldn't help him stay out of prison? What if it would actually only make sure he stayed there?"

Roberts shook his head. "I'm not sure I follow you. You're not making sense."

He continued to walk. I followed him. "He lied about his alibi, and you know it. Someone saw Tanya at the time she was supposed to be with Charles at the office. Why did he need to do that?"

Roberts shrugged. "I don't know. Lots of people lie about their alibis. Because he didn't have one? He was alone at the office maybe but thought he needed a witness to support his story?"

"But then there was the neighbor who saw his car in the driveway earlier than he claimed to be home. That's one of the reasons we took him in, remember? Why did Charles lie about the time he came home if he is so innocent?"

Roberts threw out his arms. "I had to release him, Eva Rae. We can't just keep a guy locked up with no grounds. No matter how much your 'hunch' tells us he's guilty of something."

He made air quotes around the word hunch, and it made me cringe. I hated it when people did that. My teenagers did it all the time, and it made me want to scream.

"Great, just great," I said. "And now if Charles is the one who arranged for Nancy to be attacked and for Mrs. Berkeley to be murdered, then you just put Nancy's life in danger again."

"Why do you insist on protecting her?" he asked, coming closer. "She's the one who's been lying through her teeth here. She's the one who just tried to kill someone earlier today. I hardly think she's the innocent one around here."

He turned and walked away from me. I took a couple of deep breaths, just like I usually did after fighting with my teenagers, then decided I had wasted enough time, turned around, and left.

Chapter 63

NANCY'S LAWYER took her home. It was dark out by the time they reached Merritt Island. She sat in his car, looking out the window as he drove up into Old Settlement Road and stopped.

"Will you be okay, Nancy?" Tom asked, his tone heavy.

She turned to face him. They had known one another for years, back from when she and Charles had just met. She was grateful for his help through all this. He had taken care of her, even though Charles was also his friend, or at least used to be.

"Nancy?"

She tried to smile. "I'm sorry. Thank you, Tom. For coming so fast and making sure I could go home and didn't have to stay in that awful place. Those few hours were more than enough to shake me deeply."

"You're welcome. Now, remember, you're out on bail. You can't leave town."

She nodded. "I won't."

"I'll start working on your defense case as soon as we get the charges, okay? I'll make sure to keep you out of jail. Don't worry. We'll argue for self-defense."

She exhaled. "Sounds good."

"Now, go in and get some sleep. I'll check in with you tomorrow."

"I will. Thank you."

Nancy put a hand on his arm as a grateful gesture, then got out of the car. He stopped her.

"Nancy?"

"Yes?"

"I'm sorry for everything that happened between you and Charles. I swear I didn't know what he was doing. We all thought you were dead."

Nancy swallowed. Tom didn't know it was all a lie. It still hadn't been told publicly or in the media, and the police had so far kept it to themselves. But for how long? The world was going to fall on her once they found out.

"I mean…I could…I never knew he was even capable of such an atrocious thing…to keep you, to hold you…prisoner…I'm sorry, Nance. We should have helped you somehow."

Nancy stared at him, then shed a tear. Tom would think it was because of what had happened, when in fact it was because she feared for what would happen next, once the truth was revealed.

Would she lose everything again?

"It's okay," she said. "You didn't know. How could you?"

"I just keep feeling like, I…we should have known somehow, you know? I keep going back to it, thinking there must have been some indication, something in the way he talked or acted that could have tipped us off. I should have known, and I am sad that I didn't. It breaks my heart, to be honest."

Nancy exhaled. "It isn't your fault, Tom. You mustn't blame yourself. It gets us nowhere."

He nodded with a soft smile. "I am so glad you're saying that. And again, if there's anything I can do for you, let me know."

"I will," she said, then slammed the door. She stared at the car as it disappeared down the road, heart throbbing in her chest.

Then she breathed, relieved, turned around, and walked up onto the porch.

She had already found the keys in her purse and pulled them out when she realized she wasn't alone. Someone was sitting on the porch swing, waiting for her.

Nancy turned with a gasp.

"Hello, Nancy," Charles said. "I think it's time we talk."

Chapter 64

MY KIDS WERE in the middle of a massive fight when I entered the house. I could hear them all the way into the street. It was Christine who was screaming at her little brother just as I walked in.

"I hate you so much!"

"Christine!"

I paused. She turned to look at me, then growled loudly. "What? Of course, you assume it's all my fault. Why do you always have to think the worst about me?"

"I don't, but you just told your little brother that you hate him, and we don't say stuff like that to one another. I won't have it."

Her eyes grew wide and angry, and she groaned at me. "Ugh, you're so annoying."

With that, she left and ran up the stairs, crying. I felt heavy and tired and didn't want to have to go up there to comfort her. I was beyond exhausted, and the baby was having a dance party inside my womb, stomping on my bladder.

"I'm sorry, Mom," Alex said, coming up to me and hugging me. I ruffled his hair, then smiled. "What did you do to her?"

He shrugged. "I don't know."

I lifted my eyebrows. "Really? You don't have any clue at all?"

He shrugged again, then let go of me and ran to his toys that were piled up in the corner. I glanced at the stairs, wondering if I should go up to her, then decided it would have to wait. I needed to lie down for a little while. My feet were killing me, and I was in a terrible mood. I had spent so much time on this case, yet I felt we were back to square one. We still didn't know what Nancy had been up to the past five years, and why she disappeared, if it was willingly or if she was forced to somehow. We had a neighbor that had been murdered and several attempts to murder Nancy. I had seen it myself, so I didn't doubt that someone was after her; someone wanted her dead. And now she had fired a gun at someone, probably the same person, but she wouldn't tell us who.

How were we going to help her if she wouldn't tell us who was trying to kill her?

I didn't know what was up or what was down anymore. I was beginning to wonder if I ever would—if it was even worth my energy. Maybe the sheriff's department could solve Mrs. Berkeley's murder on their own.

I sat down with a deep exhale, then shook my head. I put my feet up when my mom came in from the kitchen.

"Oh, you're home?"

She glared at my feet on the coffee table, and I sensed she wanted to say something but then decided not to.

"Yes, I just got back. Thanks for looking after the kiddos today."

She made an almost squealing sound. "Those children are a menace. The constant fighting, it drives me insane. How you are still a functioning human being is a wonder to me."

I exhaled. "Maybe I'm just very good at hiding it."

She tilted her head. "No news from Matt?"

I shook my head and closed my eyes briefly. "No, and there probably never will be. I think we're done, Mom."

The thought brought tears to my eyes. Seeing this made my mom nervous. I could tell by the way she kept rubbing her hands on the dishtowel and looking away.

"I'm sure he'll be back," she said. "I have to...I have dinner in the oven."

With that, she turned around and left the room. I looked after her, wondering why it was so hard for her to hug me or just comfort me. But it had always been her way. She had never been able to deal with me being upset or even sad. She showed her love by helping me with the kids and cooking for us. I was beginning to understand that better and better the older I got, and I appreciate her gestures, yet while secretly longing for her physical love.

"Thanks, Mom," I whispered, even though she had already left me. I leaned my head back to rest for a few seconds when a car drove up outside.

Chapter 65

I PEEKED out through the window before opening the door to see who it was this late and saw Matt. He was running a hand through his hair a few times, the way he always did when he was nervous.

For a second, I contemplated not opening the door or letting my mom send him away, but a part of me wanted to hear what he had to say.

I took a deep breath to calm my beating heart, then pulled the door open. Matt smiled on the other side. I didn't return his smile.

"Eva Rae," he said. "I have been trying to call you…"

"You couldn't take that as a hint that I didn't want to talk to you?" I asked.

He paused. His lips quivered. "You won't even listen to me?"

I shrugged. "Why would I? I don't really see what there is to be said."

"Listen, Lorraine is, was…I mean…it meant nothing. She was just someone I met at the Sports Bar."

"And so, you decided to bring her home, did ya'? Just because you're such a nice guy? Is that it?"

"No, no... I mean, yes, she wanted to…she…"

"Matt, I know you," I said, pinching the bridge of my nose. "You went to that bar, and you brought her home to…"

"I never slept with her," he said, lifting his hand. "Nothing happened."

"But you brought her home with the intention of sleeping with her," I said, shaking my head lightly.

"Nothing happened, Eva Rae. I swear."

"But it did, Matt. Something did happen. You brought home another woman," I said. "That might not be a big deal to you, but it is to me. If you don't understand that, then you don't know me at all."

He growled. "Why won't you ever listen to me?"

"I am listening, Matt. I just don't like what I'm hearing."

"God, you're annoying," he said, pointing his finger at me. "You're always in charge, aren't you? Always telling me what to do and when to do it. You're bossing me around. Yes, I took her home because I wanted to feel in control, like I was in charge for once. I guess I wanted to hurt you because I never get to be in control with you. When is it my turn to be in charge? When do I get to be important? We hang out at your house; it's your cases we work on while I just tag along. I can't even propose to you without you taking charge of that too? What's my role in this relationship? Do you even need me? Because I don't think you do. Chad really did a number on you, you know? Making you think you can't rely on anyone. Making you want to do everything by yourself. But guess what? There won't be a proposal or a marriage for that matter. I'm out."

With that, he turned on his heel and walked toward his car. I stood back, barely breathing, while he got into his cruiser and backed out of my driveway. Up until now, I had thought we could still mend the broken pieces; deep down, I had believed that there was still a slight hope for us.

But as I stared after the red taillights of his cruiser as he stopped at the end of the road before turning right, I realized I no longer believed it. After what had happened with my ex-husband, Chad, there was no way I could forgive cheating, not even if it was only a close call.

Chapter 66

THEN:

It threatened to break her...lying like that to her dad—keeping secrets from him. So many times, she was about to tell him, but then didn't because she had made her mother a promise.

Jade's stomach was acting up, and she constantly had cramps and pains. Her mother told her it was probably the hormones, or maybe because she was nervous about the upcoming exams. Her mother googled her symptoms then told her it was IBS and that she needed to eat more fiber and exercise and to stay away from sugar.

Jade promised her mother she'd eat better. No more junk.

"You have to think about your health," her mom said one day as she drove up the driveway, then pushed the garage door opener.

Another car was parked inside.

"Oh, that's odd," she said. "Your dad is home? He wasn't supposed to come back until tomorrow."

Jade got out of the car, pain growing in her stomach. It always got worse when he was home because of the lying she had to do—because she would look into his eyes and not tell him what she knew. She felt so dirty, so disgusting she wanted to hide in her bed forever.

When they entered, carrying the groceries, they found her dad sitting by the computer, his face completely pale. As she looked at the laptop, she realized it wasn't his own.

It was her mom's.

"Honey?" her mom said, her voice loud and squealing. "What are you doing?"

He lifted his gaze, and Jade took a step back. Her dad turned the screen so her mom could see.

"I would like you to explain this."

Jade stared at the messages on her mom's Facebook account. They were all from Billy. Her heart dropped, and she took a few steps to the side, then snuck out of the kitchen and closed the door behind her. She stood with her head leaned against it, panting, while she heard her mother try to explain her way out of it.

It didn't work.

"I can't believe you!" her dad yelled, and Jade jumped. "He's my best friend. How could you do this to me? Going behind my back like this?"

"I…it's nothing, honey. It really isn't…I…"

"It doesn't look like nothing. How long do these messages go back? At least a year? Have you been sneaking around on me like this for a year? Longer?"

Jade's heart throbbed in her chest. She didn't know what to do.

He'll find out you lied to him too. He'll know you hid this from him!

Jade hid her face between her hands and sank to the floor, back leaned against the door. Then she heard the words she had feared the most. They came from her father's mouth:

"I want a divorce. I want out."

"NO!" her mother yelled. She was crying now. "Please, don't say that. I promise I'll break it off with him. I won't see him again. Never. Please. I can't live without you. It meant nothing to me. I was just… lonely. Please. Give me a second chance. I know I have a problem. I'll seek professional help. Maybe if you traveled less, then we could work through this. I have wanted this to stop for a long time. I can't stand the sneaking around; I can't stand the lying. I'll talk to him. I'll tell him it's over. I promise."

Chapter 67

MY MOM STOOD in the doorway when I came back inside, a worried look in her eyes.

"Was that…Matt?"

I nodded and closed the door behind me.

"What did he want?"

She said the words, then obviously regretted them.

"Maybe it's none of my business."

"No, it's okay. You're allowed to ask, Mom," I said. "But to be honest, I'm not sure what he wanted."

She stared at me. I could tell she didn't understand. "So, you're not getting back together?"

I shook my head, pressing back tears. "It doesn't look like it."

"And the baby?"

I cleared my throat, trying to get rid of the lump that was threatening to burst and leave me to the mercy of my tears. "I…we'll have to figure that out eventually. We aren't the first ones to have to share custody."

Her eyes grew even more concerned. "It'll be tough, Eva Rae. It's no joyride having a child alone."

"I know, Mom," I said. "I have done this a few times before, remember?"

"But back then, you had Chad," she said. "There's a lot to be said about him, but he did take care of everything while you were out making that career you were so keen on pursuing."

I gave her a look. I knew she had never approved of me having a career in the first place, and certainly not now when I was alone with three, soon to be four, children. But I had to make a living somehow, and doing police work was the one thing I was good at. It wasn't exactly my plan to have another child.

"We'll figure things out, Mom. Don't worry," I said, trying to sound reassuring. I wasn't doing a very good job at it. I could tell by the expression on her face. She looked most of all disappointed. If I knew her right, I was the culprit of that. She most definitely blamed me for this. Just like she believed it was my fault when Chad left me for Kimmie. She didn't understand how much extra it added to the hurt I was already feeling. Because deep down, I kept wondering about the same thing too. Did I do this? Did I push him too far? Was he right when he told me he felt I was constantly in control and that I didn't really need him?

Probably.

"Okay," my mom said. "At least you weren't married yet and had to go through an ugly divorce. Nothing worse for a young child than to have to listen to his or her parents constantly fighting and then see them split up."

I stared at her, barely blinking. There was something I had missed —a detail that had been mentioned earlier on that I hadn't taken into account.

"They were fighting a lot," I said. "That's what Mrs. Berkeley said. That's why she didn't react when she heard them. Nancy told us they were fighting when questioned about it, but she never told us what they were fighting about."

"I'm not sure I quite follow," my mom said.

"Was Charles having an affair with Tanya already at that point? Was that why? They told us they didn't start dating until after Nancy had been gone for a while. Could it have been Nancy?" I stared at my poor mom, who had no idea what was going on at this point. "Maybe that's why she's protecting him. That's why she won't tell us who he is. That's why she said he doesn't love me anymore. That's why she didn't shoot him. Because she still loves him, while he's trying to get rid of her."

"Who's trying to get rid of whom?" my mom asked.

"I think the real question we need to get an answer to is not so much who, but why. Why will this person go so far to get rid of her? Especially if they once loved one another? It doesn't make much sense, does it?"

My mom shook her head. "None of what you just said makes any sense at all, but I am quite used to that these days. Now, if you'll get those unruly children of yours, dinner is served."

Chapter 68

NANCY'S MEMORY of pain was thin. She had gone through childbirth twice, yes, but both of her children had been delivered by c-section and she hadn't felt a thing. The pain hadn't even been bad afterwards. She had never broken a bone in her body as a child, nor had she ever been in a fight. She had once sprained her tailbone by sitting down where she believed there was a chair, but Lloyd from fourth grade removed it right as she was about to, and she tumbled to the floor instead, to the sound of the rest of the class laughing. It had hurt for three weeks whenever she walked or sat down. But that was about it, at least as far as she could recall.

Now that she was lying on the floor where Charles had thrown her after pressing her up against the wall, holding her throat, and yelling in her face, she wished she had at least some experience with pain to draw from. She wanted to say *it isn't so bad*, and *it'll be over soon*. But her throat hurt where he had held her, and her head had banged against the wall behind her.

Now, he was standing above her, panting, his hair tousled.

"Look what you made me do," he grumbled. "You make me so angry. Do you understand that?"

"Please, Charles," she said, crying. "I am sorry. I am so, so sorry."

"Yeah, well, it's a little late for that now. You have ruined everything, Nancy. Everything."

"I'm sorry," she said, her body shaking. "I really am."

"Why did you come back? Why are you lying to everyone, telling them I kidnapped you? Why?"

She shook her head, putting her arms up over her face to protect herself. Charles wasn't usually violent, but she had pushed him out over the edge. She didn't know what he might do.

"I almost ended up on death row," he spat. "I would have been killed. Are you really that cruel?"

"I...don't know," she said. "I didn't think it would go that far."

"You didn't think? You didn't think? I have lost everything because of you. My wife, my job, even the kids will barely talk to me. My reputation is ruined; I am ruined. Just because of you."

"It all happened so fast; I just...I...I'm sorry, Charles. I truly am."

"Well, it's too late for that. And it ends here. Now," he said as he grabbed her arms and pulled them behind her back. Then he grabbed a roll of duct tape and tied her hands and feet together. Nancy cried for help, but she knew it was useless.

"You're not talking to any more people, telling all those lies. My reputation is ruined; I am ruined. I am done with you. And if you think I won't harm you, think again. I have nothing to lose at this point. You made sure of that."

He then grabbed her by the shoulders and pulled her across the floor. Nancy protested and tried to fight him, but he was too strong. He had her halfway into the bathroom when they both heard a car drive up outside, then stop.

"A little late for a house call," he said, stretching his neck to look out the window by the front door. "Are you expecting anyone?"

She shook her head when they heard the sound of a car door slam shut and steps approaching in the gravel outside. Knowing this might be her one and only chance to escape, Nancy opened her mouth to scream.

Just as she did, Charles placed his hand over her mouth and held it so tight that no sound would come out. Nancy tried to bite into his hand but had no luck. Charles then pulled his gun and directed it toward the front door.

"If anyone comes through, I swear I'll shoot."

Chapter 69

I SLAMMED the door shut to my minivan, then hurried up to the front porch of Nancy Henry's house. I hadn't been able to stop thinking about it after dinner with my family and had been pacing back and forth in the living room, unable to focus on the cooking show my mom wanted us to watch.

Finally, my mom had turned off the TV and told me to either go to bed or go somewhere else. She couldn't stand it anymore. My pacing was driving her nuts. I knew I couldn't go to sleep, not with all these thoughts constantly running through my mind, trying to figure out who this guy might be. I then grabbed the car keys, rushed out, and sat in my minivan for a few minutes before making the decision. I had a bond with Nancy; we had talked before, and I felt like she trusted me —even if she didn't want to say anything after the incident at the restaurant. I now understood why. At least I was certain I did. I needed her confirmation of my theory. I hoped that by coming to her house, she might give me that, and maybe would open up to me about who he was and what had really happened to her.

It was driving me nuts not being able to figure it out.

"Nancy?"

I opened the screen door and rang the doorbell. When nothing happened, I knocked instead.

"It's me. It's Eva Rae Thomas."

I could see the lights were on inside and above me on the second floor.

"I know you probably don't want to talk to me right now," I continued. "But I need you to know that I understand now. I get why you are protecting him."

I waited to see if she had heard me and maybe would come to the door. I thought I heard movement behind the door, some kind of fumbling, but yet nothing happened. The door remained closed.

I knocked again. "Nancy? Are you in there?"

I waited.

"I promise I am only here to talk."

Once again, I thought I heard a noise coming from behind the door, and I expected it to open, but it didn't.

I put my face against the window next to the door and tried to peek inside. There were definitely lights on, and I could look into the living room, but I couldn't see anyone in there. I spotted her purse on the floor, then concluded she was definitely there but trying her best to ignore me.

I exhaled heavily.

"I know you're in there, Nancy. Just come talk to me, will you? I am only trying to protect you."

I stared at the front door.

"You love him, don't you?" I said. "That's why you won't report him."

I looked down at the door handle and placed my hand on it. I heard a sound, almost like someone talking, and stopped to listen. But then it was gone again. I turned the doorknob.

Chapter 70

NO! Don't come in here!

Nancy was sitting on the guest bathroom floor right by the front door, the one that used to have towels with shells embroidered on them and a lighthouse soap dispenser. All those things were gone now, as Tanya had removed them and replaced them with flower wallpaper and a dull steel soap dispenser instead. Charles was still holding her in a tight grip from behind, his hand placed on her mouth, the gun in his other hand pointed at the front door. She tried to scream, to yell at Eva Rae to run away when she noticed the knob was turning and almost panicked.

Nancy felt tears sting in her eyes, and the hand on her mouth grow tighter. She screamed as loud as she could, trying her best to warn Eva Rae, so she wouldn't step inside and get herself killed. But all that left her mouth was muffled groans, not loud enough for Eva Rae to hear.

The gun was shaking in Charles' hand. He was a good shot and used to go hunting with his buddies. It was one of his favorite things to do on weekends. He never missed a shot; he would always brag. Nancy knew he wasn't lying. Charles never lied, especially not to make himself look better. He wasn't that type of guy.

The knob turned, and now the door started to move to open. Nancy let out a loud squeal, and Charles pressed harder on her mouth.

"Shut up," he whispered in her ear. "Stay silent, or you both die."

Nancy was sobbing behind his hand, closing her eyes, waiting for the shot to be fired. Charles' hands were shaking heavily, and she could hear the desperation in his ragged breath. She was leaning her head on his chest and could feel it heaving up and down irregularly.

Please, God. Don't let him kill her!

When nothing happened, no shot echoed through the house, Nancy opened her eyes again to look. The door had stopped moving and was left ajar just enough to let a small child or a dog through, but not a grown person.

It stopped. Why did she stop?

Charles was sweating heavily behind Nancy, and it dripped on her forehead. The gun was still pointed at the door, the finger lingering on the trigger. Nancy could barely breathe. Eva Rae had children.

Go home, Eva Rae. Go home to your family.

The door moved again.

"Nancy?" she heard her call through the crack in the door as it slowly opened further. "I just want to chat with you for a few minutes. I know you're probably scared."

Yes, I am scared. I don't want to die, and I don't want you to die. Please, just leave. Go back!

Nancy whimpered lightly and leaned back against Charles' chest. He was breathing heavily now through gritted teeth.

The door moved slightly more to open. Nancy's eyes grew wide as she waited for Eva Rae's body to appear behind it. Charles readied the gun and steadied it, then closed one eye, holding Nancy in a tight grip.

The door moved a little more, less than an inch, then suddenly stopped.

Chapter 71

I WAS ABOUT to peek inside and call Nancy's name again when suddenly my phone vibrated in my pocket. I took my hand off the doorknob and grabbed the phone instead.

It was Christine.

I took a step away from the door and placed the phone against my ear. "Sweetie? What's going on?"

"Where are you? I can't find you. I asked Grandma, and she told me you left?" There was something in her voice that made me pause.

"Yeah, well, I had a…thing I needed to check out."

She exhaled. "Work, again, huh?"

"Yes, Christine. I have taken this case to earn a little money, so we can buy you all those nice things you like to have, and live in that nice house you like so much, remember?"

"Very funny."

"I don't really think so. What's up? Why did you need me?"

She went quiet. When she spoke again, there was a small quiver in her voice. "I need to talk to you."

"And does it have to be right now?" I asked.

"Yes."

I sighed. It really was bad timing. It somehow always was with those teenagers. "Why? What's going on?"

Christine stopped talking. I could hear her sob on the other end and realized it really was important. I stared at the door to Nancy's house that I had left ajar, then realized this could wait till later. Nancy clearly wasn't home, or she would have come to the door by now. I walked up to it, the phone clutched between my shoulder and ear, then grabbed the knob and pulled it shut. It slammed, and I hurried down the stairs toward the car.

"Talk to me, Christine," I said as I got back inside my minivan and started it up. I backed out of Nancy's driveway, then accelerated down Old Settlement Road.

"Oh, Mom, it would really help if you were here. I need to talk to you so bad."

"I'm coming back now. Try to tell me what is going on?"

She went quiet. I turned the car onto South Tropical Trail and accelerated.

"It's just, well… I shouldn't really tell you this, but…"

"Why shouldn't you tell me? What is going on here, Christine?"

She exhaled deeply on the other end. I found the bridge leading to Cocoa Beach.

"It's just…I promised not to tell anyone."

"Okay, but clearly, you need to talk about it with someone, an adult. You know you can tell me everything."

"But this is really bad if anyone finds out I've told you."

"I won't tell a soul. Cross my heart and all that…pinky promise too."

That made Christine chuckle. "I don't think anyone says that anymore, Mom."

"Well, I do. And it's very important to me, okay? I can't break a pinky promise, remember?"

"Whatever." She went quiet. I heard her sniffle.

"What is it, Christine? Is it one of your friends?"

"It's Amy."

I breathed, relieved, realizing this didn't have to do with Christine, but her best friend.

"Okay," I said as I raced past the Air Force Base and entered Cocoa Beach. "What's going on with Amy?"

Christine went quiet again.

"Sweetie?"

"She…she's pregnant."

I almost drove the car off the road; that's how bad I swerved. "She's…what? She's too young for that, Christine?"

She cried. "I know. That's why it's so terrible."

I drove up Minutemen toward my street while my heart pounded in my chest. "Christine. Who is the father?"

"She won't tell me."

"Okay. Do her parents know?"

I drove into my driveway and turned the engine off while Christine cried on the other end.

"Yes," she said through tears. "They know. And they want her to get rid of it. They want to kill it, Mom."

My heart sank as I walked through the door and found Christine sitting in the living room, her phone in hand.

"Oh, you poor baby," I said and rushed to her, grabbing her in my arms, holding her tight. At fourteen, I felt like this was a little too adult for her young heart.

"What are we going to do, Mom?" she asked me between sobs.

"There really isn't much we can do," I said. "It's up to Amy and her parents to figure this out now."

"But…she can't just…I mean, get rid of it?"

I exhaled and wiped tears from her cheek. "That's a difficult situation, honey."

"She doesn't want to," she said. "She says she won't do it. She'd rather run away."

"I sure hope she won't do that," I said. "Tell her she's always welcome at our house if she needs to. Tell me, how old is the father?"

"I told you she won't say who he is. Why?"

"I just need to figure out if a crime has been taking place. Then we have a different situation. You understand that, right? She's only fourteen."

She nodded with a sniffle. "She's actually fifteen."

"Okay. Does she have a boyfriend?"

Christine shook her head. "Not that I know of. But she did have a crush on this guy in tenth grade for like forever. They used to talk a lot."

"Do you think she was raped?"

Christine shook her head. "No, Mom, I don't."

She gave me a look, yet I continued.

"Are you sure about that?"

"I think she would have told me if something bad happened to her. We tell each other everything."

"Apparently, not everything, Christine."

"She wasn't raped, Mom. Why do you have to make everything a police matter?"

"I'm only asking."

Christine growled and got up. "No, you're interrogating. You always assume the worst. I knew I should never have told you anything."

"I am glad you did, though," I said, grabbing her arm, stopping her from storming out.

She grumbled something, then left me. I sank into a chair, trying to grasp this new information, wondering how I would react as a parent if my child came home pregnant. And if a crime had been committed? If she had been assaulted? There was no end to the anger I would feel. To be honest, I wasn't sure I would remain on this side of the law anymore.

Didn't all parents feel that way?

Chapter 72

THEN:

Jade saw his police cruiser in the driveway. Ethan stopped the Jeep and parked it behind it.

"He's here," Jade said, her pulse quickening.

Ethan placed a hand on her shoulder. "You don't have to go in. Maybe we can go somewhere else, grab an ice cream at Fat Donkey in Cocoa Beach or something. Make sure he's gone before we get back."

Jade shook her head. "No. I don't want to be scared of him. Besides, I want to see him walk out of the house after Mom sends him packing. She promised Dad she would do it today."

Ethan nodded with a smile. "I kinda want to see that too."

They walked up to the house and went into the kitchen. Ethan grabbed a soda from the fridge and threw it to her. She caught it midair and opened it. They could hear voices coming from the living room. They were loud. They both kept quiet and listened in.

"But...I can't live without you," Billy said. "You're everything that keeps me from falling apart."

Their mom sighed.

Tell him, Mom. Tell him he needs to leave and never come back. Say it.

"I enjoy being with you, too," she said. "You know this. It's all that keeps me from going insane. I feel so…trapped in this big house all day. I wish he would just let me work again."

"And we have fun, us two, right?" he asked. "We like each other."

Jade felt her heart rate go up and felt her stomach. She still hadn't figured out what to do about the baby. She had googled clinics that could help her get rid of it and decided that was probably going to be the solution. Even if it broke her heart, she was too young to have a child. Especially his child. There was no way she could go through with it. She hated him so much.

Please, just tell him to leave, Mom. Just say it.

"Come on, my love. You don't really mean that we can't see one another anymore, do you?" Billy asked, using that charm of his that Jade knew a little too well. Images of him touching her rushed through her inner eye and made her wince.

You liked it. You wanted him to touch you. That's what he'll say if you tell. He'll say you begged him to do it.

Jade closed her eyes briefly, trying to get rid of the thoughts. They were crowding her mind lately, making her doubt her judgment constantly. Was it rape? Or did she want him to? She didn't scream. She didn't say no. She just laid there, completely still, and let him…do those things. How could she ever explain that to anyone? Would they blame her for what happened? Would they look at her differently? Of course, they would. She could see just how different her brother looked at her after she had told him. Nothing between them was the same, and she wondered if it ever would be.

"We're so good together, you and me," Billy continued.

"But…my husband," their mom said. "He'll divorce me if he finds out. I promised him."

"We'll just have to be more careful then," Billy said with almost a whisper, yet still loud enough for them to hear it on the other side of the door.

Their mom went quiet, then said:

"All right. But we'll have to be very careful. No more hanging out here when the kids are home."

"I don't mind that," Billy said, and Jade could imagine the smirk on his face as the words left his lips. It made her want to throw up. Jade's eyes met Ethan's as they heard kissing sounds coming from the other side of the door. As the kissing turned to moaning and there was no doubt what was happening, Jade felt nauseated, then ran back out the front door, hand clasped against her mouth.

Ethan came out after her and held her hair as she lost her lunch to the bushes outside. She panted and leaned back her head. Her brother was shaking in anger, sweat springing to his upper lip, his nostrils flaring.

"I can't believe her. Choosing that...that rapist over her own family, over her own husband and children. I..." he paused and looked down at Jade, who was sweating heavily. "There's only one way out of this. We have to get rid of him."

"And how do you want us to do that? If we tell Dad she's still seeing him, she'll only deny it. We have no proof."

Ethan glared down at his sister's stomach. Seeing this, Jade shook her head and pulled back.

"No, no, Ethan, no."

"Yes," he said and grabbed her arms. "You have to tell Mom about the baby and who the father is. That'll make her throw him out on his hands and feet. It's the only way."

Jade felt tears spring to her eyes. "But...but she'll hate me. She loves Billy. She'll resent me for the rest of my life. Don't you understand? She'll think I seduced him or something, that I did it to hurt her."

"We'll make her understand. She has to," Ethan said and kissed the top of Jade's head. "We're her children. You're her daughter. I'll help you. I'll be there when you tell her and make sure she doesn't blame you."

Jade slumped her shoulders. She had so hoped she would never have to tell her mother about this. She could tell her mom was really fond of Billy, in the way they spoke to one another, how they teased each other, and the shared secret glances. Sometimes it even made her jealous because Billy never paid any attention to her anymore. Not since the day when he massaged her. They used to have fun and joke around. He used to smile so secretively at her and make her feel shy and special. But since that day in the bedroom, he had barely looked at her again. It had made her feel like she had done something wrong, and she often wondered if she had. Was that why he didn't like her anymore? He had told her it was their little secret when he got off her, then kissed her a last time. She hadn't kept her promise since her brother now knew. And now she was about to tell her mother as well?

Billy was going to be so mad at her. She wasn't sure she could deal with his anger or her mother's. Why did she have to be such a big disappointment?

"All right," she said, nodding. "I'll tell her."

Ethan smiled softly. He pulled her into a hug. "It's the right thing to do. And I am sure it won't be as bad as you imagine it to be. It'll make everything better. I promise."

Part IV

TWO WEEKS LATER

Chapter 73

TWO WEEKS HAD PASSED, and I still hadn't gotten ahold of Nancy Henry. I had tried to call her and even went back to the house once more, but she wasn't there. I was beginning to wonder if she had left town, even though she was told not to. The newspapers were on her case. The story about her lying about the kidnapping had been revealed, and, for a few days, it was all they talked about. I wondered if she was just hiding until it all blew over. I couldn't blame her if that were the case. A famous local politician had later been accused of sexual harassment, and soon they forgot all about the housewife from Merritt Island.

Roberts had moved on to work on another case that he had neglected, while I stayed at home to get some much-needed rest. I took care of my children and focused on them and on getting the nursery ready for the baby, even though it broke my heart to have to do so alone. I had texted a few times with Matt, but that was all I heard from him. We had a doctor's appointment coming up in a week, and I dreaded having to go to it with him. I didn't want to have to face his anger and resentment. To be honest, I was just sick of feeling lousy around him. I wanted to start looking forward to this new chapter in my life. A new life. A new baby.

Yet I still found it to be impossible to not think about the case. Mrs. Berkeley had been murdered on my watch, and I had to figure out why. I was certain her murderer was also present on that night when Nancy disappeared, and that was why she was killed. She must have seen him, I concluded. I kept wondering about the theory of him being Nancy's lover and the same guy that had tried to kill her several times after she came back. I went through Nancy's Instagram profile. She hadn't posted anything since the day she disappeared five years ago. But as I flipped through her pictures, I suddenly noticed something—or rather someone—that was present in most of them. A tall man in uniform was standing by the grill when they had a barbeque with their neighbors. He was also there when they went on a trip to the Rainbow Springs north of Orlando. He was in his trunks, standing with her children, holding a tube in one arm, and his other around the daughter's shoulders.

They were looking very familiar.

I couldn't take my eyes off the picture. Especially the look on the daughter's face got to me. She didn't look very comfortable, standing like that in a bikini with his arm around her shoulder. Something about the look in her eyes, and the way he glared down at her made me feel very uncomfortable.

I leaned back in my chair with a "huh."

It seemed almost like there were more pictures of this guy than of them with Charles. He did travel a lot, he had told us for business.

I looked at the caption for the picture. A guy was tagged in it. His name was Billy Deeks. I clicked the tag and was redirected to his Instagram page. It was set as private, so I couldn't look at it closer. But I could tell that his profile picture was of him in a uniform, a Palm Bay County Sheriff's uniform.

That was also green, like Brevard County's.

I reached for my phone.

"Roberts."

"It's Eva Rae. Do you know a Billy Deeks? He's a deputy at Palm Bay County Sheriff's Office."

"I can't say I know him, no. But I can ask around, why?"

I bit the side of my cheek. "I have a feeling we need to have a talk with him."

Roberts went quiet. "You mean he's the guy in uniform from the restaurant?"

"It's a theory, yes. Possibly also Nancy's lover."

Roberts whistled. "Really? That sounds like juicy stuff. So you think he and Nancy were lovers, and then he tried to kill her that night, and that's why she ran away?"

"Something like that. Maybe it was a jealousy fight that turned bad."

"It's a serious thing to accuse a fellow cop."

"And that's why I need you to keep quiet about it and be discreet, please. I need to be completely certain of his role in all this. We have to be very careful."

Chapter 74

"PLEASE, Charles. I can't stand this anymore. Please, just let me out of here."

Nancy sat on the floor of the bathroom in her bedroom upstairs. Charles was standing in the doorway.

"You've kept me in here for so long. Isn't it enough?"

He shrugged. "I don't know. You tell me. I sat in that cell for longer than that while the entire country screamed for my blood. You pretended to be held captive for five years. Maybe we should keep you in here for just as long, so you'll know what it was really like."

Nancy closed her eyes. She was so tired. So sick of sleeping on the floor of the bathroom or in the bathtub. Her body was aching all over, and she longed for a real bed and a real pillow instead of the towels she had used up until now.

"You don't mean that," she said. "Charles, please. You're angry. I get it. You wanted to punish me. You have succeeded. I am broken. I am tired and just want to get out of this awful bathroom. You've proved your point. You've made me suffer for what I did. Just let me out. Tell me what it'll take."

He smiled mischievously. "I want the house back. You took it from me. You took a lot of things from me, like Tanya, who won't even talk to me. But this, I can get back."

Nancy's eyes grew wide. She shook her head. "No."

"It's the price."

"Come on; you can't be serious," Nancy said. "For five whole years I walked the streets; I slept under bridges and in shelters. I would make money as a day laborer, cleaning boats and doing other odd jobs where they wouldn't ask for ID and I was paid in cash. It was an awful time for me. It's my turn to have a house to live in, and to sleep in a real bed in the comfort of my own home. You owe me this. For what I did."

He bent forward. "I don't owe you anything, Nancy. You screwed everything up for all of us. You didn't deserve any better than what you got. Besides, I'm not buying that for even a second. You were in Key West, partying."

"That's not true, and you know it. I had to struggle, working as a waitress at these awful restaurants where people groped my butt, just to make ends meet. I could have worked as a model. You know they wanted me back, but you wouldn't have it. I was used to life in first class before I met you. But you made sure to ruin that."

"You were a spoiled brat when I met you," Charles said. "But your career was going down the drain, and you know it. You should be thankful I was there to pick you up. Your beauty was fading, and you weren't getting a lot of work anymore. You were too old."

"Then why did they come to me and ask me to model for them again six years ago, huh? If I was so outdated?"

"Come on; you're not that stupid. That guy just wanted to sleep with you. And the worst part is, you would have done it."

Nancy paused. His words felt like a blow to her face. She leaned back against the toilet. "What happened to us, Charles? We used to love one another."

He stared at her, his eyes lingering on hers, and for just a second, she believed she saw something in them, a softness, maybe even affection, but it was gone shortly after.

"I stopped loving you five years ago, Nancy. And after what you have done, I hate you more than ever."

Nancy looked up at him. She felt like crying but held it back, not wanting to give him the satisfaction.

She wanted to say something clever back but never got to. The sound of the front door slamming shut below them stopped her.

Chapter 75

IT WAS HIS FAVORITE TOY. Jacob Howell had saved all his money from babysitting to buy the DJI Mavic Air 2 that he had wanted for so long. It was the best drone for aerial photos and videos. It had set him back eight hundred dollars, and his mom wasn't exactly satisfied with him spending his much money on a toy like this. Especially since she struggled as a single mom to get enough money to feed Jacob and his three brothers, but he had done it anyway. It was his hard-earned money. He loved flying the thing and taking pictures and recording video of the area where he lived. Merritt Island had so much wildlife, so many dense and impassable areas where no one ever went. There were creeks and lakes and swamp-like areas that he could get really close to, watching them up close on the display of his controller.

Today, he had taken it to Honeymoon Lake to fly over it and see if he could see any gators. He had once recorded one as it swam across Sykes Creek on the north side of the island, getting so close with the drone he could look into its eyes. A friend had told him there might be more in the lake.

He had taken his bike there and thrown it on the shore. A big gray heron stared at him like it was figuring out if he was friend or foe. Jacob barely noticed it; he was too busy looking at the screen between his hands. He let the drone slide across the lake, scanning the area for possible movement. He stayed close to the shoreline, where they might hide underneath the mangroves.

"Come on, gators, where are you hiding?"

His dad was a gator hunter. Jacob would never dare to try and shoot one, yet he had always dreamt of his dad one day coming back and teaching him how to. He had left when Jacob was only five, and he only had vague memories of him. His mom never spoke about him, and that made it harder to remember. His favorite memory was from the day when his father brought home a six-foot gator that he had killed. He had it in the back of his pick-up truck and held it by the tail while his mom took his picture, looking so proud.

That was the last memory Jacob had of him. A few weeks later, they had a huge fight, and he left, driving away in his truck.

He never came home.

"I know you're there. Come on; show your ugly faces," he mumbled while staring at the screen. He let the drone fly over a huge dense area of mangroves where it was almost impossible to see through them. He knew that would be where they were hiding, so he went really close, as close as possible, because he also had to be careful not to lose the drone. He would never get it back if it got stuck in the mangroves.

As he looked at the screen, he thought he spotted something and directed the drone back toward the area where he believed he had seen it. As it turned around and came back over the same area, Jacob realized it wasn't a gator he had seen between the crooked branches and leaves. It was something else. Something bigger. Something that was sunk halfway into the water but had gotten stuck between the mangroves. Only the top could be seen, but Jacob was certain it was the roof of a car. He found an opening in between the branches and let the drone sink down until it came close enough for him to look in through the sunroof of the car. The face looking back at him from behind the glass made him drop the controller in the water and run.

Chapter 76

THEN:

"Mom? We need to talk."

Never had Jade's heart pounded harder in her chest. It was almost painful. Ethan was right behind her as they walked into the kitchen, where their mom was preparing dinner. Jade had gone over this conversation in her mind hundreds of times and knew just what to say and how to say it, but once she stood there in person, actually doing it, she was at a loss for words. She simply couldn't remember them.

"Yes?"

Their mother's smile froze, seeing the seriousness in her children's eyes. "What's going on?"

"Maybe you should sit down," Ethan said.

Their mother grew a frown between her eyes, then did as they told her. She sat down by the kitchen table, and her children followed. Jade felt so heavy in her heart; it was hard not to cry.

"Tinks? Bubba?" she said, using the names she had called them since childhood. It didn't make things easier on Jade.

"Mom...I..."

She lost her courage and stopped. Ethan took her hand in his.

"There's something Jade needs to tell you, Mom, and it will be a little hard to hear, okay?"

Their mom exhaled, preparing herself. "Okay. You know you can tell me anything, right?"

Jade lifted her gaze and met her mom's. "It's about Billy, Mom."

Her mom pulled back, a surprised look on her face. Her eyes were suddenly avoiding theirs.

"Billy? What about him?"

Jade took a deep breath to gather herself. This was it. This was the moment she had dreaded for so many weeks. She touched her stomach gently, and her mother noticed. Her eyes grew wide.

"What is it? Tinks? What are you trying to tell me?"

Jade could hear the panic emerging in her mother's voice. She was suspecting it now, yet not ready to accept it.

"Tinks? Jade? What is it?"

Tears sprang to her eyes, even though she had promised herself not to cry. She couldn't help it. This was simply too painful.

"He...Billy...he..."

"Say it," Ethan said. "You have to. We can't let him get away with it."

Their mom clasped her mouth. Her eyes narrowed, and she struggled to breathe properly.

"Mom. Billy, he...he did things to me."

The hand was removed, the frown growing deeper. "What things?"

"Please, don't make it harder on me," Jade said. She touched her stomach again, and her mother watched with terror.

"He did things?" she repeated. "To you?"

Jade nodded.

"And now you're...?"

She let her eyes slide down to Jade's stomach and back up to her face.

"You're...you're...?

Jade nodded, now sobbing heavily. Her mother's face carried a look of utter terror as the realization sank in. Then she clasped her mouth again and began to cry behind it. Her torso was shuddering violently. Her voice was deep and hoarse as she exclaimed in horror:

"Oh, dear God. What have I done?"

Chapter 77

"I HAVE news about your Deeks guy."

I was peeling potatoes for a stew when Roberts called. My hands were slippery, and I wiped them while holding the phone between my shoulder and ear.

"That was fast."

Roberts sighed. "Yeah, well, he sort of dumped onto my desk, if you don't mind me saying so."

"Not at all. But what do you mean?"

I looked out the kitchen window at Alex, who was playing with his toy planes in the backyard. A small speedboat tugged past in the canal. It was Saturday, and my neighbors across the canal were having a barbeque in their backyard.

"Well, you're not gonna believe this, but they pulled his body out of Honeymoon River in Merritt Island yesterday. He was still in his car."

I almost dropped the phone but grabbed it in my hand instead.

"He what?"

"A kid was playing with his drone in the area and spotted the car in the water with his camera, then biked home to his mom and told her. She called nine-one-one."

I had to lean on the counter for support. I couldn't grasp this new information. How on earth did this fit into the picture? Had Nancy gotten rid of him?

"What's the time of death?"

Roberts went quiet for a second. "The guy went missing five years ago. He was last seen the day before Nancy also disappeared."

"What? That can't be true. That makes no sense?"

I had to sit down. My feet were swollen and painful today. I suddenly felt exhausted. I was so certain Billy Deeks was the guy that was trying to kill Nancy now and had hoped he was the one who had killed Mrs. Berkeley. But he went missing five years ago?

The shot. Someone fired a shot that night.

"Cause of death? Is that determined yet?"

"Yes. He was shot in the head, fractured the skull."

I pinched the bridge of my nose, trying to clear away the headache that was beginning to emerge.

"I wasn't here five years ago since I came to Brevard County only two years ago, but apparently, it was a big deal that he went missing," Roberts continued. "And get this. The Henrys were questioned about his disappearance since he was a close friend of the family. But it was never looked into deeper. They were never suspected in the case."

"And no one wondered about the fact that Nancy and Billy went missing at the exact same time?" I asked.

"It was two different departments. The investigation focused more on the fact that Billy Deeks owed a lot of money and was already under investigation for sexual harassment of a young intern at his department. They assumed he ran off because he felt the earth burning underneath him. They had some pretty hardcore evidence that he had raped the girl. He was going to lose everything."

"Wow, that's some story," I said, then thought about the pictures I had seen on Instagram, and especially the one where he had his hand on the daughter's shoulder. I knew that look in the young girl's eyes a little too well. And frankly, it gave me the chills.

Chapter 78

"Mo-om?"

Nancy's eyes flew up where they met Charles'. He straightened up, his left hand balled into a fist, hanging at his side, the other fiddling with the gun placed in his belt. He held her gaze. The spots on his neck grew darker, his eyes angrier, as if they were yelling:

Don't you dare!

Nancy wanted to yell. Hearing her daughter's voice as she called out for her almost made her burst into tears. So many times, had she dreamt about her coming to visit. She had called and called and asked for her forgiveness, but every time, she had hung up on her. Now, she was here? Actually calling out for her?

And yet Nancy couldn't answer? She couldn't tell her she was right there, sitting in the bathroom. Charles pulled the gun out of the belt so she could see it clearly while he shook his head.

"Mom? Are you here?"

Nancy bit her tongue. This was beyond hard. She wanted so badly to scream, to yell her daughter's name out, and tell her she was upstairs. But if she did, she knew she risked her life, and maybe even her daughter's. Would Charles be able to hurt their daughter? She didn't know. The man standing in front of her, glaring down, wasn't the same man she had married.

Charles placed the gun against his lips, then backed out of the bathroom and closed the door. Nancy cried, remaining soundless, and put a hand on the closed door. She couldn't believe it. That she was so close to her daughter again, and then this? What would Charles tell her? That Nancy left? Would she believe him? Would she think that she simply left her again?

There were footsteps on the stairs, approaching.

"Honey?" she heard Charles say. Nancy could tell his voice was vibrating as it did when he got nervous. "W-what are you doing here?"

The footsteps stopped. "Dad? What are *you* doing here? I thought Mom lived here now? And where have you been? We haven't heard from you in weeks. You didn't even tell us they let you out. I had to hear about it in the news?"

She sounded angry, Nancy thought. Upset.

A silence broke out. Nancy listened with bated breath. How was Charles going to explain all this?

"I came to grab some stuff; that's all," he said. "Mom's not here. I don't know where she is. I thought you didn't care?"

"It's not like I don't care at all. I mean, I am angry with her still, and even more after what she did to you, but...well, she usually calls me at least once a day to ask me for my forgiveness, and, well... I hadn't heard from her in two weeks, then figured maybe I should check on her."

"That is sweet of you, my girl, but I am afraid she has run off again."

Nancy closed her eyes and leaned her head against the door. She was going to believe him. Of course, she was. After all, her mother left her once before; why not again? Why wouldn't she take off?

"Do you think she's okay?" their daughter asked.

Nancy exhaled, relieved. Her daughter actually did care about her still, after all these years.

"I'm sure she's fine, sweetie. You know your mom. She just takes off whenever it pleases her. And she lies too. I am afraid we can't trust her. I am sorry, sweetie. It breaks my heart."

Nancy bit her lip, feeling tears pressing behind her eyes. This was more than she could take. This was the last drop.

If I live or die, I am not just gonna sit here!

Then, she did it. She did the very thing that she hadn't thought she'd have the courage to do. She yelled her daughter's name.

"JAAAADE! I AM IN HERE!"

Chapter 79

THEN:

Jade hid in her room while her mom called Billy and told him to come over. She was shaking under the covers while worrying about how this was going to end. She felt so far in over her head; it was like she was drowning.

Billy's car drove up in the driveway, and she heard the door slam shut. She went to the window and saw him walk inside. Like always, he knocked, and then opened the door, with a:

"Hello? Anyone home?"

Jade froze at the sound of his voice. Her stomach was in knots as she imagined what he would say. She kept wondering if there could have been something she misunderstood. Maybe she had done something to make him do this to her? To make him think she wanted it?

Jade walked out on the stairs as her mom asked Billy to come into the living room. Ethan came out of his room and sat next to Jade at the top of the stairs, placing his arm around her. Jade shivered at his touch, and it made him pull it back. She sent him a soft smile, and he eased up.

The voices in the living room grew louder, and Jade felt fear creep up inside of her.

"I'm telling you, Nancy. She was all over me. I am telling you the truth. I couldn't beat her off with a stick."

The sound of Billy's voice and the harshness of his words cut through Jade like a knife. Was he right? She wondered. She had asked herself that question every day since it happened. Did she want him to do what he did? Was she some kind of pervert that couldn't control herself?

"Don't give me that," her mom said, yelling just as loud. "She's sixteen for crying out loud. You, of all people, should know that's illegal. I don't care if she begged you to do it. You don't touch a kid. How could you?"

"She wanted it to happen. She's a whore just like her mom," Billy hissed.

Ethan stiffened next to Jade. His hands were balled into fists. Heart pounding, the shame growing in her throat, tears springing to her eyes, Jade whispered:

"He's telling the truth."

Ethan looked at her, mouth gaping. "I don't want to hear you say that. Not even for a second."

"But I…I think I…I liked him, Ethan. I really did like him."

"He used you, Jade. Don't you see? He doesn't love you back. He just used the fact that you had a crush on him to have sex. He thought you'd keep quiet because he knew you cared for him. He manipulated you into thinking something was wrong with you. That way, you'd keep quiet. Can't you see just how clever he has been? Making it seem like it's your fault? Making you doubt your own sanity?"

Jade exhaled. The guilt felt like it would burn a hole in her stomach. She had ruined everything.

"Besides, you have no proof I was ever with her," Billy said. "She might be making it all up. I'll deny it till the day I die. I'm a deputy. Who will they believe?"

"Except we do have proof," her mom said.

"Oh, yeah? How?" he said, mocking her.

Her mom paused for effect, then said:

"She's pregnant. I'd call that pretty darn hard proof. Don't you…Deputy?"

Chapter 80

"MOM?"

Jade shrieked. Nancy felt her pulse quicken as she heard the steps come closer. She just hoped her dad wouldn't hurt her. If he had any of the old man in him, then he wouldn't be able to. Jade was his favorite.

"Jade, no. Don't..." Charles said.

But it was too late. She had grabbed the bedroom door and opened it. Nancy heard it slam against the wall behind it.

"Where is she? Where are you? Mom?"

"In here," Nancy said, tears springing to her eyes. She moved away from the bathroom door as it swung open.

Nancy's heart skipped a beat as she saw her daughter—her gorgeous daughter—standing in the doorway, staring down at her.

"Mom? What...what are you doing in here? You...you look awful, why...?"

Jade turned to look at her dad. Her eyes fell on the gun in his belt.

"Dad? What is going on here?"

Her voice was loaded with terror.

"What's going on here? Dad?"

Charles lowered his eyes like a child at the principal's office, Nancy thought.

"Could someone please tell me what is going on here?" Jade almost squealed. "Dad? Are you holding mom hostage in here? How long has this been going on? Look at how thin she is? You can't do that!"

Charles lifted his gaze. "She put me in prison. She humiliated me. The entire world thinks I kidnapped her and held her hostage for five years in some shed. I lost the house, I lost my job, I lost my wife, and my kids. She took everything from me."

"So you decided to do exactly what you were accused of? That makes no sense, Dad."

"Maybe not to you," he said. "I told her I just wanted the house back and her out of our lives forever."

Nancy rose to her knees. "I am not giving him the house back. I was gone for five years, living on the streets or sleeping on people's couches, with no home to live in, not knowing if I'd eat the next day. I made the sacrifice to leave. It's my turn."

Charles threw out his arms. "Oh, so now you're supposed to be the hero in this story, huh? You made the big sacrifice, huh?"

Nancy stared at him, mouth gaping, tears springing to her eyes again. "I did. I did this all for my family. And you know it."

Jade stared at one, then the other. A deep frown had grown between her eyes. "What the heck are you two talking about?"

Nancy looked at the floor, avoiding her daughter's eyes. Jade crossed her arms in front of her chest. She looked from one to the other.

"I have a feeling you two have some serious explaining to do," she said and grabbed her cell phone from her jeans. "I'm gonna call Ethan and have him come here. I think he needs to hear this too. You two stay put. And no fighting, please."

Chapter 81

I DROVE up Old Settlement Road and past the Georgianna church. I noticed the flowers in the pots outside had died, withered away. Probably from the scorching sun that had burned down on us for days on end lately. We hadn't had rain for weeks now, which wasn't unusual at this time of year. The weather forecast promised showers by tonight, though, and lots of them as a low-pressure system was passing through Central Florida.

I went there alone since Roberts had moved onto another case, and I wasn't sure my hunch would be enough to make him want to spend the day on this. I was just hoping Nancy would be home. I had tried to get ahold of her for weeks, but with no luck, and now I wanted to give it one last try. She couldn't hide from me forever, and I had a feeling she wasn't going to leave town, not when she had just managed to get the house back. If my theory was correct, then I had to say I couldn't blame her for wanting to come home.

As I parked the car in the driveway, I noticed two other cars there that I hadn't seen before. I grabbed my gun and put it in the holster in my belt, then got out. The house seemed quiet, almost eerily so. There was no sound in the neighborhood—no one mowing their lawn or using a leaf blower. I couldn't even hear the birds or the cicadas, which usually made a lot of noise.

I walked up to the stairs, thinking this time she had to be home if she had company. The two cars were parked behind one another. A bumper sticker on one of them made me grab for the handle of my gun as I approached the front porch.

Chapter 82

THEN:

Jade held her breath, waiting for Billy's answer. Her mom had just told him she was pregnant. Jade had not expected her to. This made her feel worse. Would he be angry for her letting herself get pregnant? For not being more careful? After all, if she hadn't, then there was no reason for people to know what happened between them. He had strictly told her to keep it to herself. She didn't want her parents to know *what she had been up to*. Those were his words. Now, she had gone and told her mom, after all. Billy was going to be so mad at her. She couldn't stand it when he was angry.

"She's...she's...what?"

"That's right," Jade's mom said. "She's pregnant. And it's yours."

He clicked his tongue. The sound made Jade flinch. He was angry now.

"And you believe her, of course?"

"Why wouldn't I?"

"I don't know. Because she could be lying? That little whore could have been with any boy in town and gotten herself pregnant that way."

"We'll just have to get a DNA test then. That'll show who's lying and who isn't," Jade's mom said. She sounded determined, her voice saturated with disdain. "But I have a feeling we don't have to do that. Do we?"

Billy went quiet. Tears were stinging Jade's eyes. She felt like a whore; of course, she did but hearing him say it made it somehow even worse. Was that all she was to him? Just someone he could have whenever he felt like it? She had thought he cared for her, maybe even loved her. The pain was deep and threatened to tear her to pieces, rip through her stomach like a tornado. Her brother saw it on her face and grabbed her hand in his.

The silence from the living room was deafening until it was suddenly broken, and things turned for the worse. Sitting at the top of the stairs still, Jade and Ethan heard the unmistakable sound of knuckles hitting flesh. It wasn't a very loud sound and nothing like in the movies, but they didn't doubt for a second that's what it was. The scream that came after, from their mother, confirmed their suspicion.

Billy had hit her.

Simultaneously, they rose to their feet, then ran down the stairs.

The sound of more slaps and fists hitting flesh followed, and their mother's screams pierced through their bones.

"Please, Billy, no!"

They stormed into the living room and saw Billy bent over their mother, punches raining down on her. Jade couldn't breathe. Seeing her mother in distress like this completely knocked all the air out of her. Panic erupted as she feared he might kill her.

"Stop!"

The shock of hearing Ethan's voice made Billy look up. He hesitated just long enough for their mother to writhe herself out of his grip and take off sprinting for the door leading to the garage.

Chapter 83

I WAS ABOUT to knock when I heard a scream. I pulled my gun and decided to grab the doorknob and walk in. Someone was in distress. The door wasn't locked, and soon I stepped inside the living room.

"Police!" I said, holding out the gun. "I'm coming in."

There was no answer.

"Please, show yourself with hands where I can see them."

I could hear voices coming from upstairs; there was yelling and someone screaming loudly. I walked up the stairs, gun held up, sweat springing to my upper lip. The voices grew louder and angrier as I approached the top of the stairs.

"Please! Don't! Charles, please!"

The voice was Nancy's, and the despair evident. It made me fear for her life. Why was Charles here?

"I'm gonna kill you, you…I am so sick of this, Nancy!"

"DAD! NO!"

The sound of a third voice made me pause. It was female, so I concluded it was Jade's. As I peeked in through the cracked open door to the bedroom, I saw them all in there, even Ethan, the older brother.

A family meeting from hell.

I also saw something else. A gun. Pressed against Nancy's head, while she was on the floor, holding her arms above her head to protect herself as if her arms would stop a bullet. Charles was holding the gun. His face was torn, red patches on his throat and cheeks, as he yelled down at her.

"I'll finish you here and now, and it'll finally be over. Just like I should have done five years ago when you destroyed everything, Nancy. Do you realize what you have done?"

He lifted his glare as his daughter whimpered.

"Please, Dad."

"You tell her then. You tell her how stupid she was and still is. Tell her!"

"I'll tell her," Ethan said, stepping forward. He bent down till his face was close to hers. "You ruined everything, Mom. You really shouldn't have come back. You let that bastard into our lives. You slept with him. He preyed on Jade and even got her…pregnant. You're the only one to blame for what happened. You were supposed to protect her, and you let that…predator into her life."

"I said I was sorry so many times," Nancy yelled back. "How long do I have to suffer for what I have done? How long will you keep looking at me with those eyes? That look of disgust?"

Ethan snorted. "If you have come back for forgiveness, you can think again. It'll never happen. You made your bed; now you lie in it."

"Ethan!" Jade said and tugged at his arm. He turned to face her.

"What?"

"She's still our mom."

He shook his head. "I don't have a mom. It's like she's dead to me."

Ethan pulled out his gun from his uniform and placed it against Nancy's head. "And in a minute, she will be."

Chapter 84

THEN:

Jade's mom ran through the house. She grabbed the door to the garage and threw it open. Seeing this, Billy took off after her. Jade stared after them, heart pounding in her throat. As Billy disappeared out through the door as well, and they heard the familiar sound of the garage door opening, Jade turned to face her brother. Ethan was tall, yes, but scrawny. He could never take down someone like Billy if it came to it. He couldn't save their mother.

"What are we going to do?" she asked, walking closer to the door leading to the garage. From there, they could see their mother running into the driveway with Billy close behind her. He then reached out his arm and grabbed her ponytail, then pulled her back, hard. Their mother screamed, her legs in the air before she landed on the pavement. Billy then dragged her back inside.

Watching this happen, Jade stared at them, a scream caught in the back of her throat. When the garage door closed again behind Billy, her mother lying on the floor, screaming at him, Jade recoiled. She hurried back into the living room, where she hid behind the dresser, shaking heavily, clasping her mouth with both hands, holding back sobs.

Billy dragged her mother back inside and threw her on the carpet, the one they had gotten from her grandparents, that her mother hated but left out because it meant a lot to their father.

"Please, Billy. Stop," Jade's mom cried, holding her arms up to protect herself. "I'm sorry I said those things. I really am."

He grabbed her by the collar, then lifted her up, fist clenched, then hit her again, this time hard.

Jade whimpered behind her hand and closed her eyes, while Billy hit her mother again and again until Jade couldn't stand it anymore. She rose to her feet with a loud shriek, tears gushing down both her cheeks.

"Stop it! Billy, stop it!"

Billy stopped. He lifted his head and looked at her, a smirk spreading from the corner of his mouth. He let go of Jade's mother, and she sank to the floor with a deep sigh, blood gushing out of her nose, and her eyes already swelling.

"Well, well, if it isn't the little whore. You've come back for more, have you?" he approached her, coming up toward her fast. She pressed her body up against the wall behind her when he came up and grabbed her by the hips, then pressed himself up against her.

He looked into her eyes while letting a hand caress her stomach.

"You know it didn't mean anything. You and me, right? It meant nothing to me. You were just someone to help me pass the time."

He then bent over and kissed her. Jade felt like throwing up. She couldn't breathe until he finally let go of her. She sank to her knees, crying, while he stood above her, looking down at her. He was about to leave her when he stopped himself, then came back.

With a swift movement, he lifted his leg and kicked her in the stomach.

Jade gasped and fell to the floor, where he kicked her again, then again, so hard and aggressively, she soon felt the blood as it ran down her legs.

She sank to the floor, lying on her side as the child slowly washed out of her body. Out of the corner of her eye, she spotted Ethan coming up behind Billy. Between his hands, he was holding their dad's gun from the safe upstairs.

"HEY! Leave my sister alone!" he yelled.

Billy smiled, then turned to face him. As he stared down the barrel of the gun, his smirk froze.

Jade didn't even hear the gun go off. She just knew it had, right before she sank into the darkness.

Chapter 85

"I DID IT FOR YOU, ETHAN," Nancy said, looking up at her son holding the gun against her head. "You must believe me. Your dad and I agreed that I would take the fall. Once he arrived and helped us clean up, we agreed to get rid of Billy's body. He was a deputy, and we knew they'd come for you. You'd be a cop killer, and your life would be ruined. I know you hate me, but I did it all for you. I ran for your sake. You killed Billy Deeks, a sheriff's deputy. I knew they'd come for me once they found the body—when they found out how much time we spent together. All fingers would point at me, and to spare you, I took off. This way, I would never be forced to tell them the truth and ruin your life."

Jade wrinkled her forehead. "But...but, Dad...you said that Mom had just taken off and that if anyone asked, we'd have to say she disappeared. Then you told us to find alibis, to place us elsewhere on the night it happened. I passed out, I lost a baby, and you took me to your friend who is a doctor. When I came back, Mom was just gone. You said she had run out on us—that she didn't love us anymore—that she didn't want to be with us anymore. I believed you. I thought she had left because of me. Because of what I did...with Billy because it was all my fault what had happened."

"Oh, sweetie. I'd never do that," Nancy said. It hurt her heart to know that her daughter had believed such a lie. "I loved you always, Jade. It has been tormenting me for five years that I couldn't be there for you in this hard time, losing the baby and all that. I wanted to come back so terribly, but I couldn't. I thought they were looking for me because of my relationship with Billy. But after five years, I realized they hadn't even found the body."

"So, you decided to come back and disrupt everything," Ethan said. "And look at where we are now. You sent Dad to jail."

Nancy bit her lip. "You must understand; I was desperate, Ethan. I had been living without an identity for five years, without a decent place to sleep at night, making only a little here and there as a waitress, whoever would take me in without a social security number or even an address. I started to believe I could actually get my life back."

"So you faked that someone had tried to kill you?" Ethan asked. "Who does that?"

Nancy nodded. "I knew, in the eyes of the police, I had disappeared under mysterious circumstances, and that I was still a missing person's case, gone during a home invasion. So, yes, I bruised myself on the wrists, stole morphine from a doctor's office I broke into and injected myself with it, and threw myself off the bridge by five twenty, into Sykes Creek, hitting my head on the way down. It was dangerous, but I had to make sure it looked believable. I planned this for about a year and made sure there was a fishing boat close by, so they'd find me fast. It was the only way back for me."

"Gosh, that's sick, Mom," Ethan said. He removed the gun from her forehead. Nancy thought he looked so handsome in his Palm Bay County Sheriff's Office uniform. He was still in training but looked like a real deputy already.

"I thought you had forgiven me," Nancy said. "In the hospital. Jade wouldn't talk to me, but you did. I thought if I pretended not to remember anything, maybe you'd forgive me and take me back." She looked at Charles. "But you had moved on and even remarried. It was like you couldn't get rid of me fast enough. That's why I got angry and decided to frame you. When the police said they'd found that shed, I just decided to go with it and let them believe that's what happened. I just went along, and soon one lie led to another, and I have to admit I hadn't thought the consequences through, or maybe I was just happy to have one part of my old life back, the house and…well, I kind of hoped you'd come along later…because…"

"Hold on a second," Ethan said, glaring toward the door. "There's someone here."

Chapter 86

ETHAN STARED at me through the crack in the door. I had been listening in without being seen for quite some time now, and I knew enough.

"Show yourself," he said.

I walked in, pointing the gun in front of me. Ethan lowered his when he saw me.

"Agent Thomas?" Nancy asked, her voice vibrating. "W-what... What are you doing here?"

"We found Billy," I said. "I came to talk to you about that."

Her shoulders slumped.

"So, you know."

I nodded. "Pretty much, yes. The sticker on your son's car supporting the Palm Bay Sheriff's Office made me certain. He's the one who was trying to kill you, am I right? Or at least trying to force you to leave again. That's why he didn't hit you when he took the shot at you in the yard, even though it was up close, and that's why you didn't hit him either at the restaurant. Neither of you really wanted to kill the other. That's also why you said he didn't love you anymore and why you insisted on protecting him. It makes sense. We do a lot for our children. Even try to protect them from going to jail when all they did was protect their sister and mother."

Nancy exhaled. She sounded almost relieved. Maybe she was happy that the truth was finally out. It had to have been a lot to carry and juggle for one person, all those lies and secrets.

"I guess that was also why you killed Mrs. Berkeley," I said.

Nancy gasped and looked up at me.

"She was becoming a liability," I continued. "She had told you that she had doubts about whether or not it was Charles she saw that night in the yard when you were shot at."

"She came to the house the night before and told me this," Nancy said. "She also said she wasn't sure it was him in the driveway five years ago. This man was taller, she said. And he looked a lot like that guy that often came to our house, the deputy. I had to get rid of her, Ethan. I did it for you. You have come so far. I couldn't risk having all that destroyed. I wanted to tell you, but you didn't want to listen. You were just so angry all the time."

"Of course, I was angry," Ethan said. He was crying heavily now, wiping the tears off with his hand holding the gun. "For five years, we were doing so well, thinking you were gone, hoping you were dead. And now you suddenly decide to come back. Why? Because you missed us? Because you missed the house or your old life? You've once again managed to ruin everything for us."

He stood above her, then moved faster than I was able to react. He reached down and grabbed his mother by the throat, wrapping his arm around her, then placed the gun to her temple.

He looked directly at me.

"This is a family affair. Leave now, or I'll kill her."

Chapter 87

"ETHAN, DON'T DO THIS."

I stared at him, wondering how desperate he was and how far he'd take this. He had, after all, tried to kill his mother several times before. I had seen him in the house trying to strangle her.

"Put your gun down," he said. "I swear; I'll shoot her. I have nothing to lose at this point. Now that the truth is out, I am going down anyway."

He was right. I recognized that right away. A man with nothing to lose was a dangerous man. I lowered the gun, then placed it on the floor.

"Just don't hurt her, Ethan," I said.

"As I said, this is family business," he said. "Now, leave."

"Actually, when you're threatening her, that makes it my business," I said.

"Don't be smart with me. Leave now!"

I backed up, holding my hands out in the air.

"Okay, okay."

The sound of sirens filled the air. Ethan paused, then looked at me.

"What's that?"

"I called for backup when I heard screams coming from the house. It might be that. My backup."

Dragging his mother with him, he walked to the window and peeked down below. The clouds had closed on us, and a thunderclap echoed outside.

"I can't believe you did that!"

Ethan walked up to me, then lifted the gun in the air and let the grip slam down on my head. The pain shot through my body and down my spine, causing black curtains to close in front of my eyes. I sank to the bedroom floor, fighting my desire to slip into unconsciousness. I lay on the floor, gasping for air, struggling not to pass out. In the distance, I could hear someone call Ethan's name, and in the fog that was my reality, I realized it was Jade. She was screaming at him, trying to stop him.

Stop him from doing what?

I tried to get up, but my limbs refused to move. I tried to lift my head, but nothing worked.

"Ethan! She's our mom!"

Jade's voice cut through my fog, and I managed to get up on one elbow. I saw Ethan drag Nancy off, holding the skinny woman against him. I got up on my feet, conquered the dizziness and pain, then staggered after him. In the hall outside, I stopped. The sound of my colleagues coming in downstairs made me pause, then turn away from the stairs, thinking Ethan had to have heard them too. I listened and heard him down the hall, bumping into furniture. I hurried after him and saw his dark shadow silhouetted against the wall. The noise changed, and I realized he was climbing the stairs to the attic. I followed him and caught up with him as he dragged Nancy into the attic. I reached for the stairs, but he pulled the hatch closed just as I got there, and he had removed the string used to open it, so I couldn't follow him. I heard his steps above me. My colleagues came up behind me, Roberts in front.

"Eva Rae!"

"He's in the attic. He's got Nancy."

"Who is he?"

I exhaled, listening to the footsteps above. "Ethan. Her son."

Chapter 88

"IS THERE another hatch leading to the attic?" I asked Charles as we returned to the bedroom.

"Sure, there's one in our daughter's closet."

Charles showed us into Jade's old room, and Roberts pulled the hatch. The wooden ladder came down, and I climbed it, Roberts right behind me. The attic was like a musty-smelling cave and had a very low ceiling and thick beams. It was dark, and I used my phone as a flashlight.

"Help," I heard Nancy's muffled voice saying, and turned the beam in the direction of the noise.

"Over here," I said to Roberts, then stumbled after the voice while wondering if there was another way out of this attic that he could escape through. A noise made me freeze. I realized it was the sound of a ladder, one of those thin rickety metal ladders.

"He's going on the roof," I said. "He's taking Nancy to the roof."

"In the middle of a storm," Roberts said.

"Ethan?" I yelled through the darkness of the attic. "Don't go out there. It's dangerous. Come back!"

With head bent and almost on my knees, I went after him, hurrying toward the ladder leading from the attic to the roof. It was pouring in from the opening on top, where Ethan had removed the door. I couldn't see Ethan as I looked up, just the rain coming in. I grabbed the ladder and crawled up, reaching for the end with my hands, but as I grabbed it, Ethan stood there, then kicked both my hands, stepping hard on them. I screamed in pain and fell a couple of steps down before I managed to grab the ladder once again. I could hear Ethan moving on the roof, hear the bumps and thuds as I imagined he dragged Nancy after him. It had to be slippery, and I was scared they'd fall.

I crawled back up and managed to push myself out of the opening, then slide onto the roof. I wasn't too fond of heights—to put it mildly—and had to close my eyes when I accidentally looked down at the driveway with all the police cruisers below. Rain poured into my face, and I found it hard to find anything to hold onto since the roof tiles were slippery.

"Ethan!" I yelled to let him know I was right behind him. "There's no way out. You can't get away."

"Help me! Please, help me!" I heard Nancy scream.

"Stop following me," Ethan yelled back. "Or I swear I'll kill her."

Lightning struck very close by, and I screamed at the sound. It felt like the sky above cracked open. I got so frightened that I accidentally loosened my grip and started to slide down the roof. I grasped desperately for something to hold onto but found nothing. Meanwhile, the ground below seemed to come closer and closer until I skidded out over the edge. I screamed but managed to grab onto the gutter. It was a plastic one, and it bent from my weight, but it held me.

"Thomas!" Roberts peeked down at me from the edge, then reached out his hand to me, and grabbed me. He pulled me up while I squirmed in fear and got myself back onto the roof.

"That was a close one," I moaned, lying flat on the roof, not wanting even to lift my head in case I started to slip again.

"Sure was," Roberts said. "You okay?"

I felt my stomach, then nodded.

"Where did they go?"

He nodded toward the edge of the roof by the backyard, where

Ethan was standing with his mother, holding the gun to her face, holding her upright in his arms.

"Oh, dear God," I said. "If they don't fall, they'll get struck by lightning. He's gonna kill both of them, isn't he?"

I forgot all about slipping and being careful, then crawled toward them, the rain whipping my face.

"Ethan!" I yelled. "You don't have to do this. I can help."

Ethan looked down at me as I crawled up from below, staying as close to the roof as possible.

"You won't help!" he yelled back. "No one can help. No one can bring my family back. My mom broke us. She destroyed us."

"I understand your pain; I truly do," I said. "My dad…he stole my sister from me, and I didn't see her again until we were adults. It took me a long time to learn how to forgive him for that, but at some point, you have to. You can't hold onto that pain for the rest of your life."

"I'm sorry, Ethan," Nancy said, sobbing. "You have no idea how sorry I am."

He stared at her, shaking, pressing the gun against her throat. He spoke through gritted teeth.

"I don't believe you are. Not enough!"

"I am," she said, crying hard, losing herself in tears. "I am!"

"You ruined everything—all of our lives. And then you had the audacity to come back? Ever since you did, it started all over again. Why did you have to do that? You ruined everything!"

He loosened his grip, and Nancy slid to her knees, weeping. I felt terrified she'd slide down.

"I am sorry. I don't know what else to say or do. What do you want from me? You want me to die?" She looked up at him, her hair soaked, tears and rain dripping off her face. "Would that really make things better?"

Shaking heavily, he pressed the gun against her face, and she lowered her head, whimpering.

"It's all over, do you realize that? I killed someone—a deputy. That means I can never be one myself. My life is done. It's over! You did that."

"I am sorry, Ethan. What else do you want me to say? What do you want from me?"

His jaws clenched, and he bent down and looked at her. "I want you to suffer. For the rest of your life. Suffer for what you did to us."

"I already do," Nancy said. "What do you mean?"

Ethan stared down at her, then shook his head.

"Not enough," he said. "Not nearly enough. But you will."

He lifted his head, and, for a second, his eyes met mine. I realized what he was about to do, but it was already too late. A smile spread across his lips as he stretched out his arms, then started to run, setting off on the edge of the roof.

"NOOOO!" Nancy screamed helplessly as she watched him go. I grabbed her in my arms and held her down until we heard him hit the ground below.

The sound made me want to throw up.

Epilogue

TWO WEEKS LATER

I SLEPT for days on end. I was so exhausted after that day at Nancy Henry's house, and I couldn't forgive myself for not being able to stop Ethan. It tormented me. Nancy had admitted to killing Mrs. Berkeley and was kept in custody. Whether both she and Charles would face charges connected to the death of Billy Deeks five years ago was yet to be determined. They had been honest with the police during the many interviews that followed, even though Nancy was broken over her son's death. I didn't know what would happen next. It was up to the prosecutor. I had done my part and written all the reports needed. I had shut off my phone the past three days simply to give myself some peace and quiet. The baby demanded it. I could tell that I was reaching the point when I had to start slowing down for the sake of the growing child. The doctor told me so too. I wasn't in my thirties anymore, and my body couldn't cope with as much stress as when I was younger. I hated it when he said stuff like that since I didn't feel old, but I didn't want to risk anything. From now on, I was going to take it easy.

I got up and walked downstairs, still in my jammies, when I finally turned on my phone again. A tsunami of texts and voice messages overwhelmed me, and I decided to take a cup of coffee, to begin with. My mom and my sister had both been great and helped me out through this time. They had taken care of the kids for me, so I could just relax and sleep. The kids were off to school, and the house was tranquil for once. It was an utter mess with Alex's toys scattered all over the living room floor, but a little mess never bothered me. I sipped my cup and stared out over the canal. It was a gorgeous day, and the temperatures had dropped a little to the mid-seventies, and as I walked out the back door, I realized it felt extremely nice. I sat down on my patio furniture and started to go through my messages one after another. A lot of them were just mass messages from the school about upcoming drills and events.

I could easily delete them all and then move onto those that were more important. There were some from the sheriff's office about details in the investigation, but I assumed Roberts had taken care of those. He promised he would. We closed the case together and sent the material to the prosecutor's office before I pulled the plug. Roberts promised me he'd take care of follow-up questions and details that might show up while I rested. I had to assume he had taken care of it all, so I deleted them. Then came a bunch of messages from Melissa, and I read through them all, then answered her. She was just worried about me and how I was holding up—if I needed anything. I smiled when reading it. So typical Melissa. She was always taking care of me.

By the end, there was one more message, a voicemail, that I had skipped every time I got to it, but now it was the only one left.

It was from Matt.

I stared at the display, saying his name, and wondered if I even wanted to hear it. It was probably just some angry bile about how I wanted to control him and everything in our lives.

I put the phone down and decided to hear it later. For now, I wanted just to sit here, enjoy my coffee, and watch the water in all stillness. No problems, no cases to solve. Just enjoy that things were good. Not perfect, by all means, but good. The weather was nice, the coffee tasted decent, the kids were happy, at least for all I knew. What more could a woman ask for?

"There you are."

The sound of Matt's voice made me look up.

"Matt? What are you doing here?"

I was suddenly very aware that I was in my jammies and hadn't showered in days. I hoped the wind direction was in my favor.

"I called you yesterday and said I'd stop by. Didn't you get my message?"

I looked at the phone, then smiled awkwardly. "I haven't heard it yet."

He nodded and glanced out over the water, his hands in his pockets. He looked unusually handsome, and that made me feel even uglier. Seeing him again made my heart beat faster. I missed him, and I realized I had been too harsh on him. He had, after all, not slept with that woman, even though he did bring her home. Maybe it was about time I cut him some slack.

"You're in a good mood," I said.

"Can I sit?" he pointed at the patio chair next to mine.

I nodded. "Be my guest."

He sat down with an exhale. "What a gorgeous day, huh?"

I sipped my coffee, scrutinizing him. "What's with you? You're... different somehow."

He leaned back with a soft smile. "Well, I guess I have just come to a conclusion."

"I see, and what is that then?"

He looked at me. I couldn't figure him out. It was like he was laughing at me, or mocking me, or maybe just feeling a little too confident. I liked that side of him.

"That you and I can't control anything."

"That's an odd conclusion."

"Don't you see?" he said. "We've both been trying to control each other and where this relationship is going. Mostly you, but I've been doing it too."

"So, what's your point?"

He leaned forward. "That maybe it's time we just relax a little and take one day at a time. I love you. You love me. What more do we need?"

I nodded slowly, thinking that was a nice point.

"So, what are you saying?"

"I'm tired of fighting. But I can't live without you. So, I came to thinking that maybe if we loosen our grips a little, then maybe we can carry more?"

"That sounded deep. Where is this coming from? Have you been reading?"

He reached out his hand and grabbed mine in his. "I love you, Eva Rae. I am gonna try my best to be the man you want me to be, but probably fall short. I will be a good father, and I will take good care of ya'll if you'll let me."

That made me smile. "Is that a proposal?"

"I wouldn't dare to," he said.

That made me laugh. "Maybe if you try again? I promise I won't ruin it this time."

He gave me a look. "You can't order a proposal. That's not how it works."

"So, you're not going to propose?"

He shrugged. "Maybe. Maybe not."

"You've got to be kidding me."

He smirked. "You'll just have to wait and see, Eva Rae. You're not in control. Can you live with that?"

He grabbed my hands in his, smiling from ear to ear. I shook my head and laughed.

"I guess I'll just have to, won't I?"

THE END

Afterword

Dear Reader,

Thank you for purchasing NOT DEAD YET (Eva Rae Thomas #7). The idea for this story came to me when I read about a woman who had been gone for 11 years and suddenly turned up in south Florida. She had simply taken off from her family and left them, but now she was back. It was so interesting to me since I couldn't understand why anyone would ever do that. Why would you leave your family? So, I started pondering about this and concluded that the only reason valid enough for me would be if it meant that I was actually protecting one of my children from something. And just like that, the story of Nancy was born.

You can read about the other woman here if you like:
https://www.cnn.com/2013/05/01/us/pennsylvania-woman-reappears/index.html

If you wonder what happened to Christine's friend, Amy and the baby she is carrying, then her story isn't over yet. We will hear more about her in the next book.

As always, thank you so much for your great support. It means the world to me. Don't forget to post a review if you can.

Take care,

Willow

To be the first to hear about new releases and bargains—from Willow Rose—sign up below to be on the VIP List. (I promise not to share your email with anyone else, and I won't clutter your inbox.)

- Sign up to be on the VIP LIST here -

Tired of too many emails? Text the word: "willowrose" to 31996 to sign up to Willow's VIP text List to get a text alert with news about New Releases, Giveaways, Bargains and Free books from Willow.

Follow Willow Rose on BookBub:

Follow Willow on BookBub

Connect with Willow online:
Facebook
Twitter
GoodReads
willow-rose.net
madamewillowrose@gmail.com

About the Author

Willow Rose is a multi-million-copy best-selling Author and an Amazon ALL-star Author of more than 80 novels.

Several of her books have reached the top 10 of ALL books on Amazon in the US, UK, and Canada. She has sold more than six million books all over the world.

She writes Mystery, Thriller, Paranormal, Romance, Suspense, Horror, Supernatural thrillers, and Fantasy.

Willow's books are fast-paced, nail-biting pageturners with twists you won't see coming. That's why her fans call her The Queen of Plot Twists.

Willow lives on Florida's Space Coast with her husband and two daughters. When she is not writing or reading, you will find her surfing and watch the dolphins play in the waves of the Atlantic Ocean.

To be the first to hear about new releases and bargains—from Willow Rose—sign up below to be on the VIP List. (I promise not to share your email with anyone else, and I won't clutter your inbox.)

Published by BUOY MEDIA LLC

Cover design by Juan Villar Padron,
https://www.juanjpadron.com

Special thanks to my editor Janell Parque
http://janellparque.blogspot.com/

CPSIA information can be obtained
at www.ICGtesting.com
Printed in the USA
LVHW090758090221
678464LV00043B/225/J

9 781954 139824